TEXAS RANGER

Center Point
Large Print

**This Large Print Book carries the
Seal of Approval of N.A.V.H.**

WADE
EVERETT

CENTER POINT LARGE PRINT
THORNDIKE, MAINE

This Center Point Large Print edition is published
in the year 2013 by arrangement with
Golden West Literary Agency.

The text of this Large Print edition is unabridged.
In other aspects, this book may vary
from the original edition.
Printed in the United States of America
on permanent paper.
Set in 16-point Times New Roman type.

ISBN: 978-1-61173-896-4

Library of Congress Cataloging-in-Publication Data

Everett, Wade.
Texas Ranger / Wade Everett.
pages cm
ISBN 978-1-61173-896-4 (library binding : alk. paper)
1. Western stories. 2. Large type books. I. Title.
PS3553.O5547T46 2013
813´.54—dc23
2013023075

TEXAS RANGER

CHAPTER
ONE

Jim Temple had his supper in what had once been Jim East's bar, a bowl of chili beans, some crackers, and a glass of beer, and when he was through he stepped out onto Tascosa's main street, picked up the latest El Paso paper, and walked a block and a half to the jail. The town hadn't changed much since 1880, the year Jim Temple had been born; it was still a scatter of sun-baked adobe and bleached boards and dust, and if the scars on Jim Temple's face meant anything, it was just as wild and free-swinging as it had ever been.

He was the night deputy, nine o'clock to eight, every night except Sunday, when everyone was supposed to behave or was too drunk to cause much trouble. This shift, this job, this town, had been Jim Temple's for seven and a half years and now and then he got a little tired of it, tired of breaking up the fights and wrestling drunks and separating the easterners, who now and then passed through, from all the trouble they could get into trying to soak up a little of 'the wild west.'

Miles Morgan was the sheriff; he was sleeping in his chair when Temple came in, slamming the door. Morgan came awake instantly, his manner sullen.

"God damn it," he said. "How many times have I told you not to do that?"

"A couple hundred," Temple said dryly. "I'll tell you what: you catch me sleepin' on the job and you can slam the door."

"Don't get smart with me," Morgan said, hoisting himself out of the chair. He was a big man, turning fat, and at his age he'd turn into suet quickly.

"Why don't you fire me?" Jim Temple suggested.

"You can always quit," Morgan said. He went over to a sideboard and washed his face and combed his thick brown hair and gingerly put on his hat so as not to disturb the natural wave.

"Where'll I find you if there's trouble?" Temple asked.

Morgan looked at him in the mirror and smiled. "Don't bother. I pay you forty a month to handle trouble, and I've no complaints, even if you are a smart mouth." He adjusted his tie, shrugged into a corduroy coat, flicked his fingers off his hat in salute and walked out.

It rankled Jim Temple, working for Morgan, a man who played everything easy, passed out cigars and politicked all year long; he wondered why he stayed on.

Temple got his pistol and handcuffs out of the gun locker and buckled the belt around him. There was coffee on the small iron stove and he got a cup, then settled into the sheriff's chair to read the El Paso paper. Temple was long and angular, not heavy, but wiry; he was a natural horseman and had worked cattle up to the time he took the deputy's job. His face was long in the jaw and his nose was sharp, a bony ridge that had been broken twice. He had sandy hair and brown eyes and rather dark skin that hinted at some Indian blood back down the line. He was a Texan; he talked slowly, as though he had a lot of time and no ambition to hurry.

He also did not like working for Sheriff Miles Morgan.

Jim Temple sipped his coffee and opened the paper; it was early yet and although the hitchrails were solid with tied horses and the saloons were full and the stores were crowded, the excitement would not really begin until eleven.

He had two hours in which to relax.

Temple scanned the first page, then turned to the inside. An article caught his eye. Rather a word: Ranger. The article was written by a Dallas newspaperman; he was concerned with the state of the Texas Rangers. Their pay was poor: forty dollars a month for privates, fifty for sergeants, and a hundred for captains. And each man had to furnish his own horse, saddle, bed roll, arms and ammunition. He even had to pay for his own food and feed his horse.

Currently, the article went on, there were only

four companies of Texas Rangers on duty, a total of twenty-seven men. However, the governor, growing increasingly concerned over Mexican bandits along the border, and the rise of Pancho Villa, had authorized the increase to seventy-five men, and starting pay was to be fifty dollars a month.

There was a list of existing Ranger companies, and their commanders: Captain Frank Johnson, Company A, near Harlingen on the border; Captain Tom Ross, Company B, at Ysleta; Captain J. H. Rogers, Headquarters, Austin: Captain J. R. Hughes, on detachment at Amarillo.

Jim Temple got another cup of coffee and read the article again, then put the paper down, left the jail and walked four blocks to a residential street. As he went up the walk to a door, he could see Fred Almquist in the parlor; Temple knocked and Almquist's wife opened the door. When she saw who it was, she showed surprise.

"Aren't you on duty, Jim Temple?"

"Yes'm, but they don't start raisin' hob until after eleven. Could I speak with Hizzoner?"

"The mayor is in the parlor," she said and turned back to the kitchen.

Temple took off his high-crowned hat and stepped in; Fred Almquist looked up, his expression showing his annoyance. "What is it, deputy? Why aren't you on duty? Got to keep the peace, you know."

"Mr. Almquist, I've been keepin' it for some years now. Seven, to be exact. It's time for a change."

Almquist took off his glasses. "Change? What are you talking about, Temple?"

"I mean, I'm quittin', that's what. So if you'll kindly come down and open the bank so I can draw out my money, I'll bother you no more."

This was enough to make Almquist put down his book. "You'd throw away a good job paying forty dollars a month?" He snapped his fingers. "Just like that?"

"It ain't just like that," Jim Temple said evenly, "and I don't rightly feel like explainin' it either. The sheriff gets a hundred a month and fines and he ain't made an arrest in six months and the last he made were all before election time so's he'd look busy and draw attention to himself. So if I can have my money, I'm quittin'."

"You must be drunk. That's it, you've got hold of a bottle and you're drunk."

"Never been drunk," Temple admitted. "Never intend to be. I'm goin' to join the Texas Rangers."

Fred Almquist stared a moment, then tipped his head back and let the laughter boom out. He had to hold his stomach and tears ran down his cheeks and with a great effort he brought himself under control; it took a drink to fully calm him. He got up and looked at Jim Temple, then said, "Just who do you think you are? Why, the Rangers take *men*.

Do you think manhandling drunks and a few cowboys is any kind of a recommendation? Why, Temple, you'd never make the weight." He stepped close and peered at the deputy. "I've known you half your life and I'm a judge of men. You've got to admit that. I've made my fortune because of my knowledge of men. Isn't that right?"

"I got to admit that it is," Temple said, turning his hat this way and that in his hands. "But I've made up my mind."

Almquist nodded. "I can see that you have and I've never stood in a man's way. Wait until I get my hat and I'll go down to the bank with you. I assume that you have your book?"

"Yes, sir, I got it."

Almquist went to get his coat; he stepped into the kitchen for a brief conversation with his wife and although Jim Temple could not get the gist of it, he knew they were talking about him when he heard them both laugh. Then Almquist joined him at the door and they left the house together, walking along the back streets, the fragrance of Almquist's expensive cigar reminding Jim Temple that here was a man who spent a quarter on a cigar while he had to think twice before spending twenty-five cents on a meal.

Almquist's soft, persuasive voice interrupted Temple's thought. ". . . you understand that since the holdup two years ago my funds are still depleted and I won't be able to pay you back more than ten cents on the dollar. Of course, on your deposits since then—" He stopped talking, stopped walking because Temple had him by the arm and pulled him around.

"What the hell are you sayin' to me?"

"Jim, I explained this once to everyone. I lost over twenty thousand in that robbery. That was all depositors' money. Naturally, in time I'd make it good out of my own funds. After all, I gave credit to those—"

"Yeah, and Morgan served some foreclosure papers for you too. How much money have I got comin'?"

"We'll check the records," Almquist said and walked on.

The bank was a brick building and to Jim Temple, it seemed almost impossible to rob with the barred windows and doors and heavy vault inside, but it had been robbed twice in ten years; he remembered the first one because he'd been riding for one of the big outfits and they had lost their whole payroll because of it.

Almquist unlocked, went in, and made Temple wait on the customer side of the wickets. "Bank rules," Almquist said and went to the records. He thumbed through cards, then said, "Let's see, you had four hundred and ninety-two dollars in deposit when the robbery took place. The bank will make good forty-nine dollars and twenty cents. Since then you've deposited ten dollars a month regularly. That comes to two hundred and forty, plus the other." He opened a massive steel door, went into the vault and came out a moment later with the money, counting it out carefully. Then he closed Temple's account and tore up the pass book.

Jim Temple held the money in his hand and said, "Seven years work. That doesn't seem like much, does it?" He looked at Almquist. "How much have *you* made in seven years? A hundred thousand? More?"

The banker frowned. "That's a nosey question, Jim, but I'll excuse it." He put his hand on his arm and steered him toward the door, then set the lock. "I suppose you'll have the decency to tell Miles Morgan you're leaving?"

"I wouldn't want to miss the expression on his face," Temple said.

"As mayor, I can assure you that your job won't be waiting if you decide to come back."

"Why, I never did intend to come back," Temple said, amazed Fred Almquist would think of it. "Do I have to tell you what you can do with the job?"

"Someone ought to trim you down to size," Almquist said and went on back to his house.

Temple tucked the money in his pocket and walked toward the saloons and hotels and the stores doing a big week-end business. Flies and gnats buzzed around the street lights; they collected in the bottoms of the white frosted glass bowls, trapped there, dying there until the bottoms of the bowls were blackened.

He was cutting over toward the hotel when a man saw him, ran to him and took him by the arm. "Miles Morgan wants you right away. Keefer's kicking up a fuss again in the bar and Morgan wants you to take care of it."

Temple looked at his watch. "Ain't it a little early for Keefer to—"

"Oh, he ain't drunk. He's just in an arguin' mood."

"What's Morgan doin'?"

"He's havin' supper with his lady friend like he always does," the man said. "You'd better hurry, Temple."

"Yeah." He turned and walked on, ducking under the hitchrail. The hotel was ablaze with light and Temple looked in at the bar. Tom Keefer was there, a whiskered gnome of a man; he had another man shoved back in a corner and was prodding him with his finger. Temple went on into the lobby and turned toward the dining room; he knew where Morgan's table was, in the corner, half hidden by potted plants.

Morgan was holding a woman's hand and smiling, his words falling softly persuasive and Jim Temple interrupted without ceremony. "I hear Keefer's raisin' hell."

"Watch your mouth," Morgan said quickly.

Temple looked at the woman; she was in her twenties, getting hard around the mouth and long ago old in the eyes. "Thelma, you know a few cuss words yourself, don't you?" He took off his badge and laid it on the table and Miles Morgan stared at it.

"What're you doing that for? Put that back on!"

"I quit. You want to shut Keefer up, go do it yourself."

"You can't talk to me that way."

"Just did," Jim Temple said and turned away.

"Damn you! Come back here!" Morgan shouted. In the bar next to the dining room, men's talk fell off and they crowded in the connecting archway to see what was going on.

Jim Temple turned slowly and said, "Watch it, Miles. I've already quit, so I don't owe you anythin'."

Morgan had an audience now; he shoved his chair back and hoisted his bulk. The woman tried to put her hand on his arm but he shook her off and tore the napkin from his collar.

"Let it go, Miles. He's just a dumb cowboy."

"Shut up and eat your dinner, Thelma." He stepped away from the table and rolled his shoulders. "Temple, I'm sick of you."

"You want to go outside and throw up?" He started to turn, meaning to leave, to let it go this way, but Morgan wouldn't have it; he jumped, his feet heavy and he went into Temple, grappling

16

with him, bearing him down with his weight.

Temple threw all his strength into a twisting motion and fell on his side, keeping Morgan's weight off of him. Then he broke free and got to his feet and waited for Morgan. Tom Keefer was standing there, grinning. He said, "I'll give you a hundred dollars to take your place, Jim."

"I guess now money couldn't buy it," Temple said, realizing that he was going to take some pleasure in this.

Keefer said, "Fifty dollars if you can drop him with one punch."

"I'll have you in jail!" Morgan roared, pointing at Keefer. Then he looked at Jim Temple and rage built up in his eyes, thickened his voice. "I'm going to mark you up some, Temple. I'm going to put my brand on you where it'll show."

Keefer laughed again. "He's goin' to do it with his mouth, boys!"

There was a ripple of laughter and it broke the tether on Morgan's restraint; he rushed Temple like a train gone wild, his arms pumping, heavy fists trying to get at Temple's face.

Stepping back, Temple felt one bounce off his forehead and his left shoulder went a little numb, then he set himself and hit Miles Morgan, feeling his fist go into that fresh bread belly, sink in and put a big dimple in that brocade vest.

The wind gushed out of Morgan's distended mouth and his upper plate fell out and bounced on the maroon rug and he clutched his stomach and did a high-kneed dance, his step mincing. He made no sound now and his eyes bulged and his face turned blue and he kept staring at Temple and holding his belly. He fell like a large tree, rapping his head, his arms going loose.

Someone with a whit of kindness upended a pitcher of water in his face and suddenly he could breathe again, cry out in pain again; he could not get up, just contenting himself with rolling back and forth on the rug.

Tom Keefer peeled off fifty dollars and jammed it in Temple's shirt pocket. "I always thought you had it in you, boy." He winked and went back into the bar, and Jim Temple took a last look at Miles Morgan, then raised his eyes to Thelma Daniels. "You could get a real man. What do you want with him anyway?"

Then he went out and left her with his answer.

He had some packing, but not much; he went to the jail and did it, then took his canvas satchel to the depot and bought his ticket. The train for Amarillo wasn't due in for six hours, but there was a southbound in twenty minutes and he decided to take it. After all, he thought, a man could join the Texas Rangers just as well in Laredo as Amarillo.

He was sitting outside, waiting for his train when Keefer came up and sat beside him. "Someone said you was headin' this way with a satchel. Quittin' the town?"

"You wouldn't suggest I stay, would you?"

"Guess not," Keefer said. "Been smarter if I'd left too." He brought out his pipe, tamped it, lit it, puffed awhile. "Goin' back to cowboyin'?"

"Rangerin'," Temple said. "If they'll have me."

Keefer didn't laugh; he didn't even smile. "Didn't know they was puttin' on men."

"Read it in the El Paso paper." He scuffed cinders with his toe. The telephone inside the station master's office rang a few times, then stopped. Gnats buzzed around the light bulbs suspended from the station overhead. "Keefer, you say good-bye to Lotte for me?"

"A man ought to do those things for himself."

"I'll write her then, soon's I get situated." He reached into his shirt pocket and took out the money Keefer had put there. "I can't rightly take this, Tom. Fact is, I had a good bit of pleasure out of it." A whistle sounded on the prairie and Jim Temple stirred, got up gathering his canvas satchel and his rifle, a .30-40 Krag, and his saddle.

Keefer put the money in his pocket. "And I couldn't rightly afford it, but I'll just keep it for you so's you always have fifty in the sock." He offered his hand. "Jim, you promise me you'll come back. I want you to step down off that damned train with a mean look in your eye and a pearl handled pistol on your hip, you hear? And I want to watch Miles Morgan's face. I want to watch him turn to jelly."

"Hell, I ain't been accepted yet," Temple said. "You really hate Miles?"

"He's no good."

The locomotive headlight was stabbing through the darkness; the train whistled for a grade crossing a mile out of town. Keefer watched it and drew on his pipe. He said, "Last election, Morgan was all set to marry into Spindle Ranch money. As Al Shannon's son-in-law, he'd pack some weight. Then after he got elected again, they broke up."

"People quarrel, Tom."

"Yeah? And four years before that, he was sniffin' around Carlos Rameras' daughters. I admit, he wasn't engaged to any of 'em, but he had all three so hopeful that he got the Mexican vote, and there hasn't been a gringo candidate in Texas who's ever done that."

The train pulled into the station, drowning out further talk. Keefer shook hands again, waved, and walked back toward the center of town. Jim Temple got aboard and stowed his gear then sagged into a seat, accidentally bumping a passenger who had been sleeping.

"Excuse me," Temple said, wishing now he'd looked before he'd bumped. She was young, in her early twenties, and she had dark hair and large eyes that looked at him with a friendly curiosity. She saw the pistol on his hip and his rifle and said, "Going to war?"

He laughed and took off his hat and ran his

fingers through his hair and tried to think of something clever. "Already been there," he said. "Cuba. '98."

"And I'll bet you just knocked them out of the way."

"Look, I apologized. Meant it too. What more do you want?"

She smiled. "I think we're both on the edge of losing our tempers and that wouldn't be nice. I've been on this train since Sacramento and—well, it doesn't matter, really. You've got your own problems."

"If you want me to move—"

"No. If you did, some man smelling of horses is liable to sit here. I'm Martha Ivers, destination: Laredo—and marriage."

"You should have taken the southbound through El Paso," Temple advised.

Martha Ivers shook her head. "Aunt in Taos to visit. You know how it is if you have relatives."

"I don't. Had two brothers but they died in Cuba. Both got the fever. I did too but I got over it." He sagged in the seat and braced his knees against the seat ahead. "Laredo's where I'm headin'. I want to join the Texas Rangers."

"Did you know your knuckle was bleeding?"

"What?" He looked at his right hand and saw dried blood on the knuckle. "I cut it on a fella's watch chain," Temple said.

The conductor came down the aisle, taking

Temple's ticket. "Change trains in Sweetwater," he said and passed on.

"You were telling me how you cut your hand," Martha Ivers said.

Temple grinned. "No I wasn't. You was gettin' nosey when you should have been goin' back to sleep."

"Are you telling me to shut up?"

"Yep."

"All right, I'll shut up." She smiled and leaned back, closing her eyes.

He couldn't sleep; the habit of being up every night was too strong in him, so he sat there with his own thoughts, listening to the clatter and rattle of the train. It was amazing how a man could pretty much make nothing of his life. His father had wanted him to finish high school so he could become a business man, and Temple had finished, getting good marks too, only his mind had been on "rodeoin' " and "cowboyin'," and as soon as he could get on his own, he went to work for thirty a month and found, breaking horses in the panhandle.

Then Cuba came along and at eighteen and a half it sounded pretty exciting and all the girls thought it was real thrilling, so he and Ted and George had signed up. When it was over, Ted and George were dead and his father died that fall, and his mother in the spring. That always puzzled Jim Temple, for she'd been a healthy woman, but after his father had died, she just kind of lost interest in living too.

Temple decided to go into the smoking car and before he went, he folded his coat and gently lifted Martha Ivers, slipping it under her head and shoulders so she would be more comfortable. Then he left his seat and walked to the rear of the train. There were a half dozen men in the coach, salesmen mostly, men bored by too much travel; they looked around when Jim Temple stepped in.

A Negro served the bar and Temple ordered a whiskey, then turned around with it in his hand. Five men played a dull game of poker; the other one read a cattleman's magazine.

One of the poker players said, "You want to sit in?"

Temple shook his head.

"A long way to Sweetwater."

Again Temple shook his head.

The man smiled. "Afraid of losing a little money, friend?"

The colored bartender's eyes grew round. "Suhs, no trouble, tonight, suhs. A roun' on the house for you ginnimuns." He quickly set up the glasses and poured and the man reading the cattleman's journal put it down and came over to get his free one.

The poker player got up and gave Temple an elbow as he sided up to the bar. Temple looked at him, smiling, trying to keep it friendly. "What do you want trouble for?"

"I feel strong," the man said pleasantly. "Ain't

you ever felt that way, mister, like you could kick the moon, you're that tall?"

"No man is that tall."

"I am. Want me to prove it?"

"Not now. Not by me," Temple said.

"Do I scare you some?" The man was young, cocky, and pushing hard.

"Buster, all men with a loose mouth scare me a little. It means that they don't have good sense and a man without good sense can hurt somebody."

"Well now, that's some speech. I didn't know you were the windy kind." He turned around and looked at the men at the table. "Deal me in; there's no excitement around here for me tonight." He tossed off his drink and sat down again and picked up his cards. "You know there was a day when you could look at some sonafabitch and pretty well know what to expect. But those days are gone forever. Texas men are growin' tits, that's what."

One of the players said, "Be careful talkin' like that. I would be."

The young man laughed. "Hell, he just got a free drink. You can't expect a man to leave a free drink—" He stopped because the man got up and looked genuinely distressed. "What's the matter with you?"

"You're trouble, boy. I don't need any." He blocked his cards, threw them down and stepped to the bar.

He smiled at Jim Temple. "You should have come

in earlier. He almost had a fist fight over a busted flush." He took the glass and saluted, then tossed it off. "What makes all you Texans act like tomcats?"

"Not me," Temple said. "Go talk to the sore loser." He turned and looked at the poker player. "Ain't that your trouble, buddy? Been losin' a little too much?" He walked over to the table, blocked the back leg of the chair with his foot, grabbed the man by the thick hair and slammed him flat on the floor. Then he hauled him upright the same way and twisted his head back so that he looked directly at Jim Temple. "Ain't that what makes your mouth so damned big?" He waited for an answer, watching the man's alarmed, unwavering stare, then he released the hair with a shove and went back to the bar.

The Negro swallowed hard and polished furiously on the bar top. The man who had been reading the magazine seemed faintly amused. He said, "You've had some experience, friend." He fished into his pocket for a business card, and in the process he exposed a railroad detective's badge pinned to his vest. "In case you might want to take up a new line of work, we consider every application carefully. The name's Carl Hubbard. Home office, Dallas."

"I've made plans, but thanks just the same." He put the card in his pocket.

"Plans sometimes have to be changed. Keep it in mind."

CHAPTER
TWO

When the train slowed for Sweetwater, Martha Ivers stirred, then came awake. She looked at Jim Temple, then feeling his coat folded behind her head, she sat up and stretched, yawning, blinking her eyes. "You gave me your coat," she said. "Now aren't you a Texas gentleman."

"I could get people to sign affidavits that I wasn't," Temple admitted. "Feel up to somethin' to eat, some coffee when the train pulls in? We've got nearly an hour."

They got off when the train stopped and he made two trips to get all her luggage and saw that the agent had it routed right, then he walked with her toward a late hour restaurant on the end of a side street. It was a Mexican place and Temple hesitated; she looked at him oddly and said, "It's all right. I've eaten in Spanish places before."

He smiled weakly. "Here we feel some different about Mexicans. And they don't like us none either."

"You can have your likes and dislikes," she said. "I'm hungry and I smell coffee."

He opened the door for her and they sat down at

a table along the wall. When the waiter came over, Temple spoke Spanish to him, ordering for both. There were a few men in the place with their wine bottles and big hats and solitary manner. The building was adobe with a beamed ceiling, and there were only a few lights glowing. On the table there was a candle shoved into a wine bottle and Temple put a match to it.

"Like to see what I'm eatin'," he said.

The waiter brought their meal and coffee and left them alone. Martha Ivers said, "That was nice of you, with the coat. Last night I got a crick in my neck, and the night before a twinge in my back. Those seats just weren't made for sleeping." She had a rather square face and a nice mouth that was easily bent into a smile. "You never did tell me your line of work."

"Deputy sheriff," Temple said. "Seven years of it."

"That's a long time. Most men won't give up a thing after they've put that much time in it."

"No future in it," he said.

"Yes, we all put a great deal of store in that, don't we."

They arrived in Laredo in the late afternoon and they had become friends; people always loosened up on a train, talked freely, and Jim Temple supposed that it was because riding on a train was a transitory thing and a person just believed that they'd never see the other person again. He learned how she had met the man she was going to marry; a visit to California, a dance, a few quiet afternoons; those things happened and now she was in Laredo, Texas and he was going to meet her there; he was a state senator, big man in Webb County and she wanted Jim Temple to meet him, but Temple declined. He understood Texas and Texans and claimed to be in a hurry to get on with his business and said his good-byes on the train just before it reached the depot.

He got off the train before it had completely stopped and worked his way through the crowd on the cinder platform. To one side of the station he saw a shiny new car with black enameled body and polished brasswork and a smiling, full-bodied man standing up in it, trying to see over the crowd. On impulse, Temple sidled by and said, "Howdy, Senator."

The man looked at him, his smile still there. "Howdy, citizen," he said, and Jim Temple went on to the livery stable. There he rented a horse to put under his saddle, and asked directions to the new Ranger detachment. The stablehand told him that the Rangers had established a camp north of town and Temple stepped into the saddle and left the yard.

He heard the noisy approach of the senator's automobile and checked the horse, holding him under a tight rein for the noise made him skittish.

The senator wore a white canvas cap and goggles and he drove with a sawing motion of the high steering wheel, his hands working choke and spark levers to get the two cylinders firing properly. Martha Ivers sat beside him, her luggage piled up and tied on; they whipped past Jim Temple, raising dust and oil smoke, and clanked and rattled on toward the center of town.

It amazed him that any intelligent man would spend money for a thing like that, and it rather surprised him that a sensible girl like Martha Ivers would take to a man so frivolous.

The ranger camp was a disappointment; it was a cluster of tents and duckboard walks. Mexican laborers were erecting several adobe buildings; they had already built the corral. The camp was backed against a creek and shaded by a dense grove of trees; Temple rode in and dismounted. He saw several Texans supervising the work, and one of them, a rather short man in a high-crowned hat, came over. He was thick in the upper body, but his legs were short and he walked with halting, chopped steps. He wore a white shirt, dark trousers and a bone-handled .44 belted high on his hip. He was a man in his late forties, gray-eyed, with a serious, unsmiling expression.

Temple said, "Is this the Texas Ranger camp?"

"Company E," the man said. "I'm Captain Rickert."

Temple introduced himself and looked

29

around. "I guess your company's out, huh?"

"That's my company," Rickert said, indicating the two Texans bossing the Mexican workers.

"Two men?" Temple asked.

"I started with none," Rickert said. "Come on in my tent."

He turned and led the way; there was a cot and a small wooden chest and a writing desk and Rickert's personal gear piled in one corner. "Sit down, Temple. What's your problem?"

"I wanted to join the Rangers, Captain."

"Any experience in law enforcement?"

"Seven years. Deputy sheriff in Oldham County."

Rickert frowned. "Under Morgan?"

Jim Temple smiled and scratched the back of his head. "I was afraid that wouldn't help me any, but I'm bein' honest when I say that I did the work and he won the elections."

"Why didn't you run against him?"

"No ambition," Temple admitted.

George Rickert studied him for a moment. "Well, that's honest. In time I'm going to put together a company here, seventeen men. But joining the Rangers isn't just a matter of walking in and getting a badge. We want good men, the best we can find. There are five others coming here; they've written me and asked for appointments. I don't play favorites, so you'll take the same examination they do. I'm going to give it Monday morning. You can stay in town. How are you fixed for money?"

"I've got my savings," Temple said. He got up and didn't offer to shake hands; Rickert somehow didn't hold with it. He went out and Rickert followed him to the livery horse.

"If you're accepted, Temple, we'll train you. You'll have a head crammed full of Texas law. We'll know all we need to know about you. Suit you?"

"Sure," Temple said, "and thanks."

Rickert smiled and his face turned pleasant. "For what? For a job that'll make an old man of you by the time you're forty? For poor pay and terrible meals and a Mexican bullet from ambush? Temple, that deputy's job is going to seem like vacation in comparison."

"I know what I want, Captain." He stepped up, turned the horse and rode back to town. At the livery he turned the horse into a stall, paid the hostler, then walked five blocks to the hotel and registered there. He was getting his key when a hand touched him lightly on the shoulder and he turned his head and looked at the gambling man he had roughed up on the train.

"Small world, ain't it?" the man said pleasantly. He was young with a shotgunning of freckles across his nose.

"Be careful you don't crowd anybody then," Temple advised.

"I'm glad I ran into you," the man said. "I really made a jackass of myself on the train, didn't I?"

He grinned foolishly. "Don't know what the hell got into me. Never done anything so stupid before. But you did me a favor, mister."

"How?"

"It never hurts a man to get cut down to proper size." He wiped his hand across his mouth. "I'll tell you what if you won't laugh. I came down here to join the Rangers. No background for it, really; I clerked in the railroad freight office. But a man gets the notion he's tough. You know. I saw you and I tried to lean against you. That was stupid." He offered his hand. "The name's Sanderson. Fred Sanderson, but everybody calls me Sandy. No hard feelings?"

"Not as far as I'm concerned," Temple said. "You been out to the camp yet?"

"You know where it is? Say, you're not going to join too, are you?" He slapped Temple on the shoulder. "Let me buy you a drink."

"Can't refuse that," Temple said and went with him to the hotel bar. Sanderson ordered whiskey, but Temple wanted beer and Sanderson changed his order too. They took their steins to a table and sat down. Temple leaned his shoulder against the wall and stretched his long legs.

"I've been thinking that maybe I'm too young for the Rangers," Sanderson said. "I won't be twenty-five until fall and pa always said that a man didn't have a lick of sense before he was thirty."

"How much did you lose at poker on the train?"

"About forty dollars." The humor left his eyes. "Before I left home, pa said—"

"It seems like your pa does a lot of sayin'," Temple interrupted. "Why don't you forget what he's said and do what you say? Huh? Ain't you old enough to make up your own mind?" He laughed and winked. "I'm gettin' a little nosey now, but how much could you really afford to lose in that game?"

"Not forty dollars," Sanderson admitted. He due into his pocket and counted his remaining assets. "About thirty-five dollars and some change. Well, if I bust out here and don't make it, I'm not going back and have them laugh at me. A man's just got to keep on going, don't he?"

"I've already taken a room here," Temple said. "You could share it with me. I can use the company. Strange town and nothing to do but kill time. We can swap lies."

He said it just right and Sanderson lifted his stein of beer, clacking it against Temple's. "I swear I won't even snore."

Monday morning they had breakfast at six o'clock and were out to the Ranger camp before seven, although the examination was not going to be given until eight. At that time, Captain Rickert provided a long table and camp stools beneath a shade tree. Four other men had showed up. Three

33

of them were range-bred; the other was a city man, in a gray suit, flat-heeled shoes and a soft felt hat.

Rickert passed out pencils and papers, saying, "Answer all the questions; don't skip any. If the question does not apply to you, write: 'none,' in the blank." Two more men arrived and this annoyed Rickert, who had to explain it all over; he was a man who liked to say a thing once. "There'll be no talking, no whispering, and no getting up to pee. You've got two hours to complete the job, so get going."

The examination contained a detailed personal history that went back three generations; Temple filled it out and went on to the other parts. There was a goodly section on Texas geography and the applicant's knowledge of cattle, horses, brands, homestead laws, laws of arrest and seizure, firearms, customs regulations. As Temple kept sharpening his pencil and writing, he realized that Captain Rickert had made up this examination himself, using it as a way of knowing quickly all he could about the applicants.

Temple finished his and Rickert took it; he leaned against the bole of the tree and read it, now and then making marks on the margin. Finally he collected the papers and said, "Go on over to the cook fire and help yourselves to coffee. I'll call you in one at a time."

One of the Texas Rangers handed out tin cups

and poured from a blackened pot; he was a grave-faced man, tall, and heavily armed. His cartridge belt was wide and contained both .30-.30 rifle cartridges and .44's for his revolver, which was perched on his left hip, cross-draw style, in the skimpiest holster Temple had ever seen. There was a back piece of saddle skirting, but the entire weapon was exposed, except the tip of the barrel, which rested in a leather cup. Spring tension on the top of the frame and under the trigger guard held the Colt in place.

The Ranger saw Temple's curiosity and said, "Fella in Dallas makes these rigs." Then he dropped his hand, turned his palm out, and the spring popped and the .44 was in his hand, ready for serious business.

"Well, for Christ's sake," Temple said. "That's about as slick a rig as anythin' I've ever seen."

"Use it with either hand too," the Ranger said. "And it's snugly held. A fall or a horse pitching can't shake it loose." He stopped talking because Rickert came out of his tent. "Pete Andrews?"

"That's me," the city man said and handed his coffee cup to Jim Temple. "Mind that for me, will you friend?" He grinned and dashed off toward the tent.

The ranger said, "My name's Ed Hurley and I wish you fellas a lot of luck. You're the second batch that's gone through. The old man's pretty fussy."

"You mean," Sandy said, "that he didn't pick anybody yet?"

Hurley nodded. "Well, he will. You fellas look pretty good to me. It's no job for a man looking for somethin' easy. They come here with the idea of struttin' around with a badge and a lot of authority. It shows in a man and the captain don't want that kind. A man's a Ranger because he wouldn't have anythin' else. The pay's terrible and the hours are long and you're damned lucky if you get three days vacation a year." He jerked his head to indicate the other Ranger supervising the Mexican workers. "Jake Collins and I have been in about six years. We'll train you, if you make it with the captain, and when we're through, you'll be as good as any man in the service."

Pete Andrews came out; he walked slowly back and took his coffee cup from Temple; he seemed a little dazed. "I made it," he said, then his moon face split into a grin. "I'll be a sonofabitch, I made it!"

Another man was called; he was in only a few minutes then came out, got on his horse, and rode away. Two more followed and left the camp. Sanderson licked his lips and glanced nervously at Temple. "What the devil do you suppose he's looking for anyway? Those fellas looked all right to me." He let his glance swing to Ed Hurley. "I don't suppose you'd tell a man?"

"If I knew, I would," Hurley said.

"Temple," Rickert called and was waiting inside when Jim Temple stepped in. "Sit down. In looking over your application, I see that you've done a good job of answering some of the more specialized questions." He put the paper down and studied Jim Temple a moment. "Pete Andrews is acceptable but there's a lot he doesn't know. If I were to accept you as a Ranger, would you be willing to teach him, in addition to your own duties? This would mean damned little sleep for you; you'd have to carry him on your back for awhile. Would you do that?"

"I guess I would if you asked me to."

"Would you volunteer for it?"

Temple thought about it for a heartbeat. "Yes, sir, I'd do that."

"I don't suppose I can get much of a recommendation from Sheriff Morgan where you're concerned."

"No, I guess you won't," Temple admitted.

"What do you suggest I do then?"

"That's up to you."

"Then I'll tell you what I've already done," Rickert said. "When you came out last week, I wired Morgan. He sent a letter down to me and by his say-so you aren't fit to be a dogcatcher. Do you want to read it?"

"No, sir. A man makes up his own mind who he wants to believe."

"That's exactly right," Rickert said. "So when I

read the letter I thought to myself, now here's a man who puts it on damned thick. I've written adverse reports on men and I make it short and to the point; I don't go on for five pages." He kept watching Temple, boring holes in him with his eyes. "I sent two more wires. Al Shannon of Spindle says you're a good man, and Carlos Rameras of Spur says he's never heard anything bad about you. I think you'll do for us, Private Temple. I think you'll do very nicely."

He let out his breath in a gush and didn't try to hide his relief. Then he said, "Captain, you still want me to help—"

Rickert shook his head. "A Ranger stands on his own feet. I wanted to know if you would, when there wasn't anything in it for you. In the Rangers we'll ride through hell with a tin cup of water to put out the fire if another Ranger asks us to. If a man won't risk his life for a saddlemate, he's not fit for the service, not fit to ride with. That'll be all, Temple."

"Thank you, Captain."

"Temple, within six months you'll be in here begging me to quit."

After he went out, Rickert called Sanderson in and Temple winked at him as they passed in the yard. When he came back to the fire, Ed Hurley said, "Well, you didn't get on your horse so I guess I'll be makin' a Ranger of you."

"Yeah, you got your work cut out."

• • •

Pete Andrews, Temple, and Sanderson were picked; the others were dismissed. Captain Rickert came out of his tent and the recruits stood in a row in front of him. "If you gentlemen have any personal business in town to settle, I suggest that you do it. From now on in you are bound by rules and regulations. You are recruits in the Texas Rangers. In three weeks you will be privates, paid forty dollars a month. You will provide your own clothes, guns, ammunition, horse, saddle, and you'll feed yourself. When you eat at the company mess, you'll pay thirty-five cents for it, just like a restaurant in town. If your horse is killed, the State of Texas will buy you another at the going rate. Recruitment is left up to the captain of each company. In this company there will be seven men, not counting myself. Sergeants Collins and Hurley are in charge. Training is left up to the captain, and personally I like to turn a man to duty when he knows what he is doing. I will give you instruction in the law, powers of arrest, and matters like that. The sergeants will instruct you in marksmanship and horsemanship. A Ranger, by reputation, rides like a Comanche, shoots like a Kentuckian, and fears no man or beast. And I'll have no man in my company tarnish that tradition. In the Rangers you go where you're sent, often alone, and you do your job and rejoin your company. Sometimes that won't be for a year or two, but you're always a Ranger. Good people look up to you. Bad ones fear you. The Mexicans hate you, and a Ranger soon learns not to ruin his voice yelling for help because there usually isn't any. We don't wear a uniform and we don't want one; people have learned to look into a Ranger's eyes and identify him; that's the kind of men we breed, proud men, strong men, men who can't be bought off or frightened off. We have never had a man who betrayed his trust or neglected his duty to Texas or another Ranger. And we won't have. A Ranger must be able to stake his life on the courage and integrity of a saddlemate. When a man says, 'I'm a Texas Ranger,' he is saying that he is unflinching in his duty, beyond corruption, beyond personal opinion. A Texas Ranger stands for law and justice. Often he stands alone, against a mob, against inflamed tempers and unreasoning acts. And he can't lose his head, or his judgment. There was a day when it took a company of Rangers to put down trouble, then our reputation spread until one man could do it. Often now the very threat of bringing in a Ranger will quell trouble. We don't have three hundred men in the service. We don't even want one hundred. We want quality; we demand it and we get it. Now some of you don't have proper gear: a good horse, weapons. If you lack the finances, we have a company fund that you can draw on and pay back at twenty dollars a month. A Ranger rides a fine horse and carries weapons that are in good repair. He is familiar with these weapons. We encourage shooting contests. We encourage practice and more practice in getting your weapons into play with the least amount of lost motion. We do not like to hear of a Texas Ranger ever beaten to the draw by anyone but another Ranger. I'll turn you gentlemen over to your sergeants. That's all. Dismissed."

They were taken to tents and given cots and a wooden locker to stow their gear; the three recruits shared the same tent and Sergeant Hurley said, "You got fifteen minutes to get settled. The rest of the day is yours to settle your business. Tomorrow you belong to the State of Texas."

Within a week it became clear to Jim Temple that every one of them—Sanderson, Andrews, and himself—possessed a good deal of knowledge on certain subjects. Because Sanderson had worked five and a half years for the railroad, his knowledge of Texas geography was phenomenal; there was not a whistle stop or water tank that he couldn't identify, and his mind was filled with railroad schedules and telegraph stations; he knew the name of every dispatcher and stationmaster, and he could work a telegraph key with some proficiency.

Pete Andrews had worked six years for a large cattle buyer and his mind was a file of names, brands, locations; if there was one branded cow in the state that he didn't know about, Temple felt sure that someone was keeping it in a barn with a blanket over it.

Jim Temple understood the procedure for arrest almost as well as Captain Rickert did; it had been Temple's job to know the law—city, county, and state—and during the first week he was required to share this knowledge with the other two. Each man was trained, and he helped train the others until they all were knowledgeable, all efficient, and Rickert was a big one for tests; hardly a day went by they didn't give each other tests.

They bought horses in town; Jim Temple paid two hundred and fifty dollars for a long-legged bay with the chest of a runner, and he'd learned enough about a really suitable firearm from Jake Collins to know that his old .38-40 just wouldn't do. So he traded in his .30-40 Krag for a '95 Winchester .30-06, and Collins helped him pick out a .44-40 with a five and a half inch barrel. Temple liked the cavalry model with the long barrel, but he was learning when to use a rifle and when to rely on a handgun, so he took Collins' advice.

A saddlemaker, under Collins' specific instructions, made a holster and cartridge belt for Jim Temple, and it cost him nearly forty dollars, but the first time he drew the gun he knew it was money well spent. He liked a pistol riding high and firm, on his right hip, drawing with his right hand and he got a rig like Collins had, open all the way down the front, the gun being held in with a spring; a man just whipped it out with only the slightest lifting motion.

It seemed to Temple that they were always riding or answering questions or shooting or practicing something; finally it came to an end and he looked at Sanderson and Andrews and they were not the same men who had first come to the camp. They dressed in duck trousers and shirts and their boots were always dusty, and their hands and face had been burned mahogany by a constant sun. Yet it went deeper than appearance; they were thinking like Rangers now, feeling like Rangers, confident, ready for anything that lurked around the bend.

They were ready for an assignment and Captain George Rickert had one.

CHAPTER
THREE

Jim Temple wasn't sure where he got the notion, but he had it firmly set in his head that they would be working together; of course it was stupid, once Captain Rickert gave them their orders. Sanderson and Jake Collins saddled horses, loaded a pack mule and rode south toward Rio Grande City, working the border because the Mexican bandits had been very active there, and there was a good deal of gun running in that locality since the Mexican bandit, Zapata, was building an army.

Jim Temple wouldn't see either of them for over a year.

Pete Andrews and Sergeant Hurley took the train to Hebbonville; there was a flurry of oil drilling in that part of the country and a dispute had flared up into open shooting; Captain Rickert wanted it put down and no time wasted doing it.

Jim Temple stayed in Laredo.

In reply to Rickert's continual requests, the State of Texas enlarged his company by five and after the usual screening, he took in that many recruits, and it became Jim Temple's duty to help train them. In order that the recruits learn the tenets of respect for authority. Temple was made "jawbone" sergeant; no increase in pay but he had the authority.

This was not the duty Jim Temple had hoped for, but he showed Rickert none of this disappointment. Rather he dug into his work with a determination to produce the best batch of recruits George Rickert had ever seen.

And his dedication was not wasted. If a recruit did a thing well, Jim Temple was not satisfied until the recruit could do it better, and he had a knack of making the recruit discontented until he did it better.

Horsemanship was becoming less important to a Ranger; there had been a time when great skill was a commonplace thing, but that was changing; a man could take a train to just about anywhere and a two hundred mile chase across country was rarely done in the saddle any more. Recruits were presumed to be horsemen of some ability; every male Texan was expected to ride, and a good deal of his duty was performed on horseback, but a Ranger put his horse in a cattlecar, rode to his destination, unloaded the horse there and mounted up. So his training consisted of proper care of animals, packing, and trail riding.

The recruits were not permitted to leave the camp, but now that the permanent buildings were finished, life at headquarters was pleasant. The adobes were laid out in a square around the supply and headquarters building, in the fashion of a small military post, with a main gate, a parade ground, a stable gate and yard, and a water gate leading to the creek.

The recruits lived in a barracks, but Temple, as a sergeant, rated a room to himself, comfortably but simply furnished, and the thick adobe walls kept out the summer heat.

It was his privilege to go into Laredo after duty hours, but since the recruits couldn't enjoy this privilege, he remained in camp, going into town only on Saturday night, or on Sunday, and then it was only to order supplies for the Mexican cooks. In addition to his training duties, he also acted as liaison between the border patrol officers, the local constable, and the police magistrate; there was a good deal of commerce and traffic back and forth across the river, and since every province in Mexico was breeding a revolutionary army, the demand for firearms and ammunition was enough to inspire illegal shipments, and keep the border patrol very busy.

Temple left the Ranger camp late Saturday night, rode into town with a dispatch case full of messages for the sergeant in charge of the bridge inspection station. He delivered these, gossiped for a half hour, then went to the bank to get the Monday payroll, and afterward stopped in at the general store to place the commissary order; he would come in in the morning with a wagon to pick it up.

Before he left town he met the city marshal making his appointed rounds and they went to his office, which he shared with the constable, and had a cup of coffee.

His relationship with these men in allied trades was cordial, yet oddly proportioned; the town marshal made slightly more than double Temple's salary, and he was married and had three children in school. The constable, who acted as jailer and officer of the court, earned only slightly less than the marshal. Yet each of these men always deferred their opinions to Temple's because he was a Ranger and they were merely local officers, and seniority had nothing to do with how much money a man earned.

It was, he supposed, his jurisdiction; the State of Texas was his beat; his authority was the governor's authority, vested in him, that made citizen or judge listen when he spoke.

So Jim Temple took great care in what he said and because of this, found that his normal stream of conversation was cut in half.

After his coffee, he took a turn around the main street, meaning to go back to the Ranger camp, but there was a dance at the hotel, and the beat of the music and the laughter and bright lights pulled him to the outside fringes of it, and he stood on the dark side porch and looked in through the window.

From his right, in the shadows, a woman

said, "Why don't you go on in, Jim?"

He started; he hadn't seen her there, then he looked closely and made her out; Martha Ivers was sitting in a cushioned porch swing. Temple moved over to where she sat and leaned against the railing. "I'd think your dance card would be full," he said.

"I also like the cool breeze. How have you been, Jim?"

"Busy. How's married life?"

"Oh, I won't know that until late October."

"If I was your man I wouldn't wait that long."

"Yes," she said. "I know. Ranger Jim Temple. I think it has a nice sound to it. Like it?"

He nodded. "It suits me to a tee." He turned as a large man in a dark suit came out, drinks delicately held between thumbs and forefingers; he seemed annoyed to find Martha Ivers and Temple talking, but he smiled, handed her the drink, then turned and looked at Jim Temple.

"I don't believe we've been introduced," he said.

"Lon, this is Ranger Jim Temple. Jim, Lon Barrett, my fiancé."

"Senator," Temple said and shook hands.

"I'm certainly happy to have this opportunity to make your acquaintance, Mr. Temple, so I could thank you properly for the kindness you showed to Martha on her journey here. She's spoken of you several times, and although I don't approve of young single girls traveling alone, I was thankful that she had fallen into the care of an honorable Texas gentleman."

This barrage of words rather buffeted Jim Temple; he was accustomed to men saying what they meant with more economy, but he supposed it was that way with people in politics, an ability to say no in two hundred words without batting an eye, and leaving the refused with the impression they'd been done a favor.

"To tell you the truth, senator, I sat down beside her and didn't even see her until I'd gouged her in the ribs with my elbow." He smiled and took out his tobacco and rolled a cigaret; in the flare of the match his face was lean and darkly tanned; his mustache was dense but closely clipped, filling his upper lip, finishing his face so that one's lasting impression was confidence and character. "Miss Ivers tells me the wedding is going to be in October."

"Yes indeed, and it'll be a grand affair. The governor will be there, of course; I thought I'd rent an entire floor of the hotel. A woman deserves a memorable event, you know. After all, she's only going to get married once." He sipped his drink. "May I get you something?" He put his drink down. "Allow me. I certainly owe you one."

He turned and dashed back inside before Temple could protest or stop him; he was the kind of a man who seemed to leave behind him a swirl of wind, a disturbance, a wake, a memory of his passing that was not easy to forget.

"He sure talks up a storm," Temple said, then wished he hadn't said that because it sounded like a criticism and he hadn't meant it that way at all.

"You should hear him on the floor of the senate," Martha said. "I hear that he can talk for an hour and not say a thing." She put her hand to her mouth and giggled. "He does sound pretty pompous but it seems to impress the voters. Jim, will you come to the wedding?"

"If I'm here," he said. "Once these recruits are turned into the company, I may get an assignment. And there's no way of knowin' where it'll take me." He looked inside, peering through the window. "I wonder what's holding up the senator?"

"The bar's pretty crowded," Martha said. "He may not be back for ten minutes. Jim, I've thought about you. Is that bad?" He could see her face vaguely; she was watching him. "You just popped into my life and then disappeared. Is joining the Rangers like going into a monastic order?"

"Pretty near."

"Somehow that doesn't quite fit the picture I have of you. I mean, you seem like a man who'd have a girl to take to the Saturday night dance and the ice cream social on Sunday."

"I used to do things like that," Temple admitted.

50

"But to tell you the truth, I never could afford a steady girl until I took that deputy sheriff job, then it seemed like all the girls I took a shine to were spoken for." He smiled, drew a final drag on his cigaret and shied it onto the lawn. "You ever know a man who gets everywhere late?" He tapped himself with his finger. "That's me."

"Now I just don't believe that," Martha said. She turned her head as Lon Barrett came out with a whiskey and soda.

Jim Temple spent another fifteen minutes with them, then excused himself, got his horse and went back to company headquarters. He expected to find Rickert's office darkened, but there was a light on and while Temple was putting up his horse, Rickert came to the stable.

"Stop in at the office," he said and went back.

When Temple got there, Rickert was reading some reports; he motioned toward a chair and when Jim sat down, he said, "Do you know this man?" He spun a telegram across the desk. Temple read it and nodded.

"Tom Keefer. Yes, I know him well. He's a good man. Sometimes a little too independent for his own good, but honest as the day is long."

"As you can see, that wire was forwarded to me from the company at Amarillo. I got it in the mail, along with a letter of explanation from Captain Hughes; the whole matter is in his territory and he would normally handle it." Rickert tipped back his chair and laced his fingers behind his head. "Before we move in we must have a request from the local law. Hughes has had no such request. Besides, he's short-handed and since Keefer mentioned you, Hughes wanted my opinion."

"Keefer would tell the truth. It's got him in trouble, especially with Miles Morgan."

"If it's true, then it ought to be looked into," Rickert said. "According to Hughes, the bank was held up last Wednesday afternoon, just moments before closing, and it was nearly cleaned out, a little over eighteen thousand dollars. Up to the time he wrote the letter to me, Sheriff Morgan had made absolutely no progress at all in picking up the trail of the robbers. Top that off with Keefer's accusation that the whole thing was a put-up job—" He unlaced his fingers and spread his hands. "So I'll wire Hughes tonight and tell him I'm putting you on the job. Catch the first train north. Straighten it out. Clear Morgan if he's in the clear, but if he's doing anything out of line, run him out of office. Clean it up, Temple."

"Yes, sir."

"I'm going to leave you on the books as a jawbone sergeant. Someday, if you keep your nose clean, we can make it permanent."

"Anything that suits you, captain," Temple said.

"I want to hear a noise from that part of the country, Temple. You know what I mean? I want answers. I want a clean county."

"Yes, sir. Will that be all, sir?"

Rickert nodded. "I'll finish up with the recruits. If you need help, whistle." He got up and offered his hand. "Good luck. You know the law; use it. And I'll expect regular reports."

He was dismissed, and he went to his quarters and packed a few spare shirts and socks, his razor and soap and towels, and rolled it all into his bedroll. He was about to take this to the stable when Rickert knocked on his door and came in. He laid a two-shot .41 derringer on the dresser and said, "A man can drop this in a boot or put it in his hat or strap it to his arm; and it may give him two more shots when everyone thinks he's cracked the last cap in the carbine."

"Thank you, captain. I'll take the loan of it." He put it in his shirt pocket and buttoned the flap.

Riding north was not the same as his trip south, and it was not a matter of direction; it was a state of mind. He was heading north now with the authority of Texas in his pocket, in the leather folder which contained his identification and badge. He was going back, looking for trouble this time and he knew Miles Morgan wouldn't like it. Neither would Fred Almquist.

Yet Jim Temple didn't feel like rubbing anyone's nose into anything; he had his job and he meant to do it, quietly, efficiently, completely so that his final report would close the matter and reflect no tarnish on the reputation of the Rangers.

He changed trains again at Sweetwater and saw that his horse was grained and watered, then he slept in the chair car section until the conductor came through, hawking the next stop in a strident voice.

Temple got down and helped unload his horse; he saddled in the shade of the depot and the station agent came out and watched him, but said nothing. Finally Temple mounted and looked at the agent from beneath the shaded brim of his hat. "How have you been, Charlie?"

"Tolerable, Jim." He looked at Temple, at the heavy, shiny blue rifle in the scabbard and the pearl-handled pistol in the spring holster and the enormous belt of ammunition, enough ammunition to supply a platoon, and he said, "I reckon the sheriff is takin' the mornin' sun on the hotel veranda." Then he smiled and let old friendship show. "There was some that said you'd never make it."

"I made it," Temple remarked and turned his horse toward the main street.

There was no change in the town; he hadn't expected any; the street was as dusty as ever and would stay that way until the first rains, then it would turn into a mire, alternatingly wet and dry and finally freezing into deep ruts. Temple walked his horse three quarters of the length of the street, making no move to draw attention to himself, but getting it just the same. He could see the word go on ahead of him, the arms being poked and the heads turning. Then he stopped in front of the bank and swung down, the huge Mexican rowels jangling as they dragged at each step.

There was a small crowd by the bank door; he nodded to them and banged his knuckles on the oak. The men watched him, saying nothing, then Almquist spoke from behind the door. "Who is it? Go away! Can't you see the bank's closed?"

"This is Sergeant Temple, Company E, Texas Rangers. Open the door."

There was the moving back of one of the curtains, then the bolt was shot and Temple stepped inside. Immediately the crowd by the bank surged toward the door and he turned and put out his hands, bracing them on each side of the door frame. "Ain't you got anythin' better to do than to stand around in the hot sun?" He looked at one man, singling him out. "I never knew you to make trouble for anyone, Silas. Poor time to start, ain't it?"

He waited and they looked at him, tall and browned in his tan shirt and pants; he was friendly but he was firm, resolved, completely sure of himself and suddenly they were no longer sure of themselves.

Silas Ridenhour said. "All right, Jim, now that you're here, we'll leave it to you. But a lot of backs are against the wall this time. And no foolin'."

"I never thought anyone was foolin', Silas." He stepped inside and closed the door, then looked at

Fred Almquist, a nervous, worried man. Almquist looked like the man who had bid five dollars for the first prize pie and then found out that his wife had baked it.

He said, "Who asked the Rangers to step into this anyway?"

"Let's go into your office," Temple suggested. He waited a moment, waited for Almquist to move, then he took the man by the upper arm and dug in his fingers and propelled him along slightly ahead of him. When he turned Almquist loose, the man jerked his sleeve as though to snap out the wrinkles.

"By God, I'll report this to your captain!"

"His name is Rickert. Laredo." He sat down and brought out a small notebook and a pencil. "Will you give me the details of the robbery?" He looked steadily at Fred Almquist. "If you'd rather, I can have the grand jury convened and a subpoena issued."

Almquist shook his head. "It was near closing time—within a few minutes of it. I was about ready to lock up when three men came in. One walked over to the teller and—"

"Who was behind the cage?"

"Ken Wallace."

Temple wrote it down then nodded for Almquist to go on. "The man asked Wallace how he would have to go about transferring money from a Dallas bank to mine."

"Describe the man."

"Oh, five-foot eight. Sandy hair. I didn't pay much attention."

"What did the other two do?" Temple asked.

"One filled out a deposit slip at the counter by the south wall."

"What'd he look like?"

"About six-foot, very thin. I never did get a good look at his face."

"Why not?"

"I was talking to the third man."

"Describe him then."

"Medium high, rather moon-faced. He wore a duster and a derby and had a mustache, thick, like yours. The next thing I knew, the wall clock struck five and Wallace let out a groan and fell to the floor. I looked at him and saw that the man he'd been talking to had hit him on the head with a gun barrel. Then the man I was talking to shoved a gun in my ribs. They tied me, cleaned out the vault, and walked out the front door." He wiped a shaking hand across his face. "I would have yelled but they'd gagged me. Wallace didn't come around for a good fifteen minutes but I'd worked my hands loose by then and made it outside."

"How much did they get?"

"Eighteen thousand, one hundred and eight dollars. They cleaned me; I've had to close the bank."

Temple kept writing. "When you gave the

alarm, did anyone come forward and say that they'd seen the three men and the direction they took out of town?"

"No," Almquist said. "Well, not exactly no."

"What does that mean?"

"A couple of men loafing across the street said they saw the three men pass the bank. They walked west, went into Ben Perch's saloon."

"After robbing the bank?"

"That's what I figure they did," Almquist said. "It does sound funny, doesn't it?"

"What does Perch say?"

"He says they helped themselves to some free lunch and then asked to use the back room for a minute; and then when they didn't come out, he went back to look for them but they'd gone out by the back door."

Temple went on writing. "When they talked, was there anything distinguishing about their voice? Any scars or anything like that you'd remember?"

Fred Almquist shook his head. "No, nothing."

"I'll want to talk to you later," Temple said, putting his pencil and notebook away. "Thank you for your time."

"You're wasting yours," Almquist said, and walked to the door to open it. "Those three are in Arizona or Oklahoma or some place by now."

"How did they get there?"

"How in hell would I know? All I'm sure of is that they got my money."

He locked the door after Jim Temple stepped out. There was a good crowd jamming the walk across the street, but the side on which the bank stood was clear, at least right in front of it. Temple turned and walked toward the hotel, unmindful of the people ahead who clogged the walk, blocking his way. He did not slacken his pace and it seemed that he would walk right into them, but at the last moment they parted and he passed through without brushing any of them.

Miles Morgan was sitting on the veranda, his chair tipped back, his hat brim resting on the bridge of his nose. He moved his eyes, looked at Jim Temple, then said, "Get out of my county. No one invited you here."

"You know why I'm here," Temple said. He mounted the steps and casually knocked Morgan's feet off the railing, making his chair bang forward on its legs, making him lose his hat. He picked it up, dusted it, then set it on the back of his head. "Where can we talk?" Temple asked. He kept his voice down, kept it pleasant. "I'd like a report of your investigation."

Without making much noise at all fifty people crowded around the veranda, standing there, hands in their pockets, listening. Miles Morgan said, "Why don't you all go home? What do you expect a man to do anyway?" He blew out a long breath. "All right, they didn't take the train and no one remembers seeing three strangers on horses and they didn't have one of them automobiles so you tell me how they got away!" He looked from face to face. "Come on, tell me if you're so all-fired smart!" Then he waved his hand and looked at Jim Temple. "You think I haven't done my job? Sure, that's what you think." He got up and set his hat more firmly. "All right, let's go to the office. I'll give you your damned report. And I want to see you find something I've missed."

He bulled off the porch and roughly made his way through the crowd and cut across the street, Jim Temple following him. Inside, Morgan opened a desk drawer and flung a thick sheaf of papers across the desk. "There you are, sergeant. Statements. Three dozen statements from every-one who saw the men. All written out in black and white. They just up and disappeared. No train, no horses, no automobile; they just flapped their arms and flew away with all the money. Now you just show me anything that I've missed and I'll eat that file."

"The money's gone," Temple said. "There has to be answers, Miles."

"Find 'em! Go ahead. You always made out that you ran my office anyway. Go ahead. You tell me." He eased his bulk into his chair and the rungs creaked beneath the weight. "I'm going to turn the whole thing over to you, Mr. Smart-ass Texas Ranger. But one thing I'm sure of: no man could have investigated this any better than I did."

CHAPTER
FOUR

After breakfast, Jim Temple rode out of town to the Keefer place, a six-hundred acre farm split by the confluence of two good creeks. Keefer had built on a wooded rise: house, barn, sheds, and hogyards; he'd built that way because there had been a time when a farmer was a pox in cattle country and the high ground had given him a clear view of any hostile approach.

Lotte Keefer was feeding the chickens when Jim Temple rode in; she put down her pan, ran to him and jumped up, clasping her arms tightly around his neck so that her feet hung clear of the ground. She was a mite of a girl, flaxen-haired and as shapely as a peanut; Temple swung her around and put her down. Then Tom Keefer came out, suspenders dangling; he hitched them up with one hand and shook hands with the other.

"Now if you ain't good to see." He winked. "But I guess Lotte's told you that already. Come in and sit. Just finishin' my breakfast." He turned and led the way into the house and Temple followed; Lotte walked with him, her arm around him.

There were times when Temple just didn't know

what to make of her; she was so outgoing that it embarrassed him. In age, she was nearly ten years younger than he, and he supposed it all started years before when he had given her a ride on his calico pony; she'd sort of affixed herself to him ever since, in a friendly way.

Keefer sat down to finish his ham and eggs. "Can't be like most men," he said, by way of explanation. "I got to put in two hours work before I eat. Don't seem right somehow to get up from rest and eat." He waved Temple into a chair and Lotte poured him a cup of coffee. "By golly, Jim, it's good to see you again. Would you do somethin' for me? Would you let me see your badge? Just once?"

Temple reached into his hip pocket and laid the badge on the table; Keefer didn't touch it. He just examined it carefully and said, "Ain't that somethin'? Lotte? Ain't that though? By golly, a man that carries that is some punkins. He sure is."

Temple put the badge back in his pocket and leaned back in the chair. Lotte sat across from him and leaned her chin in the cup of her hand, smiling, watching him. "I made papa write the letter. I told him it was his duty. We didn't have any money in the bank, but it was still his duty."

"I lost plenty the last time it was robbed," Keefer admitted. "Now I take care of my own money. I don't get Almquist's interest, but I don't get robbed either. People don't pay much attention to me, I'm happy to say. They don't pay much attention to any of us farmers, but we make out. Yes, sir, in the run of it, we make out better than the cattlemen do. It's hard for 'em to see that though. They make their money in a lump, when they ship, and they just don't stop to add up the dollar here and the dollar there that the farmer makes. But they buy hay and they eat the vegetables from Lotte's garden and the bacon in their bellies comes from my hogs. That's the way a farmer makes it, here and there, chickens, eggs, crops, livestock, and I'm not fool enough to put my money in Almquist's bank."

"The captain thought you wrote a pretty interestin' letter," Temple said. "What ever gave you those notions, Tom?"

"Facts," Keefer said. "I ain't stupid. I can count to ten and if I have to go higher, I can always take off my boots. First off, Fred Almquist came from Oklahoma Territory, from around Ardmore. I looked into the matter thorough-like, and he had a bank there, only it got robbed, cleaned out, busted."

"How do you know this?"

"Lotte's ma come from that part of the country. She's still got kin there that I'm friendly with. Fact is, when Almquist went busted there, Lotte's ma was alive and I loaned her kin four-five hundred dollars. Paid me back too. That's the kind of people they are."

"All right, so Almquist lost everything in Ardmore. Go on."

"Five months later he shows up here with ten thousand dollars and opens up a bank right across the street from the Cattleman's Trust." He made a disgusted noise. "Citizens Savings Bank, my hind end! Where did he get ten thousand? He'd lost everything in that robbery in Ardmore."

"He could have borrowed it."

"Could have, but he didn't. I'll bet my life that if you examined his books you'd never find interest paid out on a loan of that size." Keefer shook his head. "I'm just a farmer, but I know somethin', Jim. Let's just talk round numbers to keep the figures in our head and you'll see there's a heap of money in the small town banking business. Say you've got ten thousand and you decide to open a bank; you list that as capital assets and open the door. Suppose there's another bank in the town; right off you've got to cut into the competition, so you make short term loans to cattlemen, secured by beef sales for four per cent, two cents cheaper than the bank across the street. Then you offer five per cent on straight savings accounts."

"Sounds like you're losing money."

Keefer smiled and shook his head. "At this point the banker has put out about three or four thousand, but in ten days he'll have it back through depositors who just can't turn down that extra one per cent interest, and a lot of them will take accounts out of the old bank and put it in the new."

He paused to light his pipe, then he went on. "Now the banker can use his depositor's money and keep his own in the sock, and as soon as the cattleman ships, he'll get the money he loaned back, plus the interest. And you've got to keep in mind that this bank is owned by one man; all the profits are his. So, now's the time for him to make a smart move; he makes a bunch of small, bad-risk loans, loans that were turned down by the bank across the street. He gets all the security he can: land, equipment, stock, crops, but if he can't really cover the loan, he makes it anyway. The interest will be fifteen or twenty per cent, but the amounts are small, usually no more than three or four hundred dollars. But it builds business, Jim. It brings depositors in to cover these loans should any of 'em be paid off. In a year the banker is sittin' pretty; he has a good reputation and he sings in the church choir or sits in on the council meetings. Maybe he'll run for office. Of course, he's been talkin' poor weather and poor crops and falling market prices and he's cut the depositor's interest back to three per cent and hiked loan interest a little higher, but he's not hurting any. The bank across the street is hardly making out and there's talk around town about the new one buying out the old."

Jim Temple said, "Tom, I didn't know you knew these things."

"I make a study of what interests me, and I've been interested in this for six years now. In three or four years, the banker has made more money than you or I'd care to count. He foreclosed on considerable land and owns town property, got the same way. And he sits on this, holding the price up so that no one will buy it. You've seen Fred Almquist do this. But it's for a reason, Jim. A very important reason. Let's say that he has twenty thousand of his own money now, and another sixteen thousand in the vault. He also owns property worth an actual seven thousand, but shows a market value of twelve. The plum is pretty ripe, just about to fall off the tree, so what does the banker do? He arranges to have his bank held up, cleaned out. The robbers get away, and of the sixteen thousand that's taken, the robbers get four thousand, and the banker gets twelve." He held up his hand to keep Temple from interrupting. "I ain't done. All right, he's got twenty thousand of his own and another twelve that belongs to depositors. Right off the bat he squeezes to collect what loans he has outstanding. After all, a terrible thing has happened and he wants to protect the depositors. Of course he had some insurance, say about ten thousand, and he collects that, which brings the total to forty-two. Then he 'sacrifices' his property for eight thousand total. You see the kind of money we're talking about? Now this banker loves the community and feels a strong debt to the depositors, so what does he do? Why, out of his own pocket he pays out every cent, one hundred cents on the dollar, a total of twelve thousand dollars. Are they happy? Jim, you remember when Almquist did that. They made him mayor at next election and there wasn't a man in town who'd think of running against him."

"He damned near doubled his money," Temple said.

"More like tripled it."

"I don't follow that."

Keefer laughed. "When the depositors found out they weren't going to lose their savings, they went and left the money in the bank. After all, it was safe, wasn't it? The banker made it good, didn't he? It's a case of: 'If you ain't got it, I want it, but if you have got it, I don't.' Almquist paid back that money full value because he wanted to set them up for the next robbery. How did it turn out two years ago, Jim? Fifty cents on the dollar, and a year later another ten cents. By my figures, Almquist came out a good thirty-five thousand to the clear on that one. The thing workin' for him is that people need a bank, Jim; they just can't do without one any more. If a man wants to buy some land, he has to go to a bank generally to have the matter handled, for the loan and things like that."

"You believe Fred Almquist had his own bank robbed three times?"

"Four. Don't forget the one in Ardmore."

Jim Temple scratched his head. "I lost money in that robbery. I'll never get it all back either. Tom, you really believe Almquist set this up?"

Keefer nodded. "I've been askin' a lot of questions and made my conclusions. Now you ask your questions and then you come to me with what you figure out. We'll see how they add up." His coffee was cold, but he finished it and got up. "I got work to do. Fetch him another cup of coffee, Lotte; it won't hurt him to keep you company a spell." He grinned, pulled up his suspenders, grabbed his straw hat and slammed the screen door.

Lotte got him his coffee, then said, "Pa sure gets wound up, doesn't he?"

"I never knew him to go off half cocked on anything," Temple admitted. "Some years back he swore up and down it was the Quinn boys who were makin' off with Al Shannon's beef. Turned out that way too, didn't it?"

She sat down again and watched him, smiling. He said, "Lotte, what do you do that for?"

She wrinkled her nose. "I like you, Jim. I used to tell myself that when I grew up you'd marry me."

Her honesty surprised him and he laughed. "Well, you believe in comin' right out with a thing, don't you?" He shook his head and spooned sugar in his coffee. "As you can see, I wouldn't be much of a prize. On my pay all I could afford would be one room with a stove and a bed in the corner."

"Have you been thinking about it?"

"Oh, now don't get me backed into a corner, Lotte."

"I'm not trying to do that," she said. "But pa says that a man needs a woman. Pa says that if a man can't have the right woman, then he turns to ones like Thelma Scanlon, who've neither toiled nor spun."

Jim Temple laughed. "The cracker barrel philosopher. But I guess he's right. That's what makes your pa so damned hard to get along with sometimes; he's generally right and people hate to be caught wrong. And Tom was never again' rubbin' a man's nose into somethin'."

"You always got along with him. How come?"

Temple shrugged. "Because he was an old tom turkey who shines no man's shoes, I guess. I respect him."

This pleased her; he could see that in her eyes. She was a pretty girl, delicate boned, with fine skin undamaged by constant sunlight, and it seemed that her waist was almost small enough for him to span with his hands, yet he knew that she was woman enough; it was a feeling he had, a knowledge that came unbidden, unsubstantiated.

"Have you got a girl in Laredo?"

She was always surprising him that way; he

said, "Well, I met one going there on the train. Seen her a couple of times."

"Don't tell me about her," Lotte said. "I hate her already."

"You don't hate anyone, Lotte."

"No," she said very quietly. "It isn't in me, I guess." Then she looked squarely at him. "But I love you, Jim. I guess I'd better say it while I've got the chance; you're just apt to up and leave like you did the last time and—" She found that she couldn't go on with it; she folded her hands and bent her head and looked at them as though she were praying mightily. "Please give me a chance, Jim. Please?"

He pushed back his chair and got up and came around the table; she seemed weightless when he lifted her, planted her feet on her chair. Then he wrapped his arms around the round warm firmness of her buttocks and squeezed her to him and she wiped tears away with the back of her hand and tried to smile, tried to be gay and carefree again. He held her taller than he, as though she weighed nothing; she had to look down at his face and she put her hands lightly on his cheeks.

"Oh, say something," she begged.

"You're a pest," he told her, smiling.

"I know it."

"You've been a pest since that day I gave you a ride on my pony."

"I only asked you because I knew you'd put your arms around me to hold me so I wouldn't fall." She laughed and wiped her eyes again. "You were so handsome and you could roll cigarettes with one hand."

"I always said that if a girl had to fall for a man, that was as good a reason as any. Want me to put you down?"

She shook her head, still smiling. "Uh, uh."

"You know, I waited a long time for you to grow up, then I suddenly realized how old I was and—"

"Oh," she said softly, "that's not old."

"If your pa comes in and sees me holding you like this he's goin' to think somethin' funny's goin' on."

"I don't care. What is going on, Jim?"

"For a long time I've been wonderin' when I should stop treatin' you like a little sister, and now you've told me." He set her lightly on her feet.

"What did you do that for?"

"Because I've got to go, but I'll be back." He checked his stem-winder. "I can make Al Shannon's place in two hours. Supper time all right?"

"I'll have the things you like best."

He smiled. "Lotte, you know so much about me. Is that good?"

"I like to think of it as a head start on any other female."

"Practical," he said, winking. "Good kid."

71

She took his arm when he tried to turn. "Hey, you haven't kissed me."

"Well, I was going to save that for—"

"There's other things to save," she said and wrapped her arms around his neck. She stood on her tiptoes and put her mouth to his and he felt a shock slam through him. It was the kind of kiss a wife gives her husband when the kids are asleep and she's just had her bath and figures he's spent enough time with the newspaper.

When they drew apart she put her hands to her cheeks and said, "Oh, wow." She didn't put any particular emphasis on it; she said it rather breathlessly, as though her discovery had been full of wonder, her reward boundless beyond her imagination.

"With a little effort," Temple said, "I'll bet I could walk out to my horse and get on the first try." He put his arm around her and pushed open the screen door and walked with her that way across the porch.

Tom Keefer came from the barn; he cast his pitchfork into the manure pile and when he came up, Lotte said, "Jim's coming to supper, papa."

"Figures. Never hurts, talk." He glanced at his daughter. "Your cheeks are a mite flushed. Been standin' near' the stove, I expect."

"Someday," Temple said pleasantly, "you're going to see somethin' and hurt your eyes." He laughed and stepped into the saddle, backed his horse, and rode out of the yard.

This was his country; he knew every creek, draw, wash, waterhole, fence line, road, trail, line cabin and he cut across Keefer's place to a southwest corner gate, let himself through into Willis Parker's farm, hit the road and passed on toward Spindle range.

He came to a gate and a warning to rustlers and trespassers; he bent in the saddle, pulled the latch and rode through, making certain the gate was securely fastened before riding on. He followed a low hogback for over a mile then he saw a crew working in a long swale and headed there. They were branding, and the noise and dust was thick; over thirty riders worked the herd, and as Temple came close enough to be recognized, Hobo Teal, Spindle's foreman rode out to meet him.

He sat his horse, hat cuffed back to expose dark, Comanche hair. Teal wore a lot of silver on his hatband and belt, a throwback to his Indian grandparentage, but he had blue eyes and freckles. He smiled at Temple, raised his right hand and said, "How, Jim."

"And how, Hobo." He looked on at the branding. "Early shipment this year?"

"Yeah, the market's good and the old man wants to let go some of the two-year-old stuff." He crossed his hands on the pommel. "A Texas Ranger no less. I'll be dogged. It makes a man half jealous." He heeled his horse into motion and rode slowly around Jim Temple, whistling softly at his armament. "I don't guess I've ever seen a man so well heeled. Care for a little draw and shoot?" He jerked his head toward the camp. "Cookie's got some tin cans. Say ten cents a can and the loser buys the cartridges?"

"Sure," Temple said and rode back with him. He didn't particularly care for this sort of thing, but he understood why it had to be because he'd worked cattle, known the boredom, the danger, the tedium, and after awhile it was anything for a change, a break, something to laugh about or talk about later. Men of the saddle were full of humor; it was a contrast, a necessary balance to their lives, and every cow camp had its champion pistol shot or calf roper or bucking-horse rider.

Work stopped when Hobo Teal and Jim Temple rode in; he knew all of these men, by name, and by reputation. Some wood was thrown on the fire to keep it hot and Teal said, "Jim's agreed to a little draw and shoot, so Smokey, you fetch some cans from the cook—"

The man already was trotting toward the chuckwagon and Hobo Teal went to his bedroll and got his holster and belt. He came back, tying it down through a pair of holes in the batwing of his chaps. The cans were being set up a good ten paces away, a neat row of six.

Teal said, "How about if cookie bangs a pot for the signal? All right with you, cookie?"

It was, and it suited Temple.

The idea was to draw and shoot, bouncing as many cans as you could before the other fellow got in his shot. The cowboys gathered around, grinning, cracking the dust on their faces; sweat ran down their cheeks, making muddy furrows and when they moved their arms, dust broke loose from the weave of their shirts in small, constant clouds.

Teal went into a crouch, waiting and Jim Temple stood there, his arms loose, relaxed, then the cook rapped the pot with a spoon and he drew, snapping the .44 free, firing as the muzzle came up. He bounced a can and another, then stopped because Hobo Teal wasn't shooting.

"Now what the hell kind of sneaky is that?" Teal asked good naturedly. "The echo of the pan bangin' ain't gone and you've got off a shot."

"You want another chance?" Temple asked.

"Yeah, and this time, wait for the signal."

One of the riders said, "He waited, Hobo."

"When I want you to say somethin', I'll ask you. All right, cookie, whenever you're ready."

Temple had replaced the spent cartridges and reholstered his gun; he drew on signal, in one fluid motion, letting the hammer roll out from under his thumb as the muzzle came in line and he bounced two cans, and a third just a split second before Hobo Teal's shot went into the dirt where the can had been.

"I'll be plumb go to hell," Teal said and paid a dollar and fifty cents for the five cans and ten cents apiece for the shells. Then he looked past Temple to the crest of a rise and took off his gun and put it away.

Al Shannon rode into the camp and dismounted. "I heard shooting," he said. "Howdy, Jim." He saw Temple punch spent brass out the loading gate. "Oh, a little shoot-off, eh? How'd you do, Hobo?"

"Terrible. The Rangers have taught him nothin' but dirty tricks." He grinned and immediately went back to work, not concerned with what Shannon would have to say about the time out; Shannon understood range bred men and would be sorry he'd missed it.

Temple and Al Shannon walked to one side, away from the worst of the noise and dust; they sat on the sloping side of the rise; their horses grazed nearby. Shannon was nearly sixty, a tall, proud man with a mane of gray hair and a long waterfall mustache, quite out of style on anyone but him.

"One of my men was in town yesterday," Shannon said. "He said you'd come back." He took out a cigar, and a knife, snipped off the end and lit it, being careful with the match in the dry grass. Then he used his boot heel to dig a hole in which to dump the ash. "From the looks of things, the bank's going to stay closed. And I don't suppose Morgan's turned up anything?"

"No, he ain't, but I've got to give him credit for tryin'."

"He was out asking me a lot of questions. The main road to the west runs through my property; he wanted to know if I'd seen anyone pass that was a stranger. As it happened, I'd put Teal and a crew to work out there, four days steady, settin' new fence posts and stringin' wire. They had about four miles to set and I'd bet money that a rattlesnake didn't belly along that road but what they saw it." He flicked ashes from his smoke. "Matter of fact, the boys took rifles along and blew the heads off a few jack rabbits. Made the cook fix 'em too. Tough, stringy varmints. Beats the hell out of a man. You hire the best cook in six counties, pay him extra wages to keep him on so the men won't growl, then they want to eat jack rabbits just because they shot 'em." He shook his head at the wonder of it all. "So I'll say to you what I said to Miles Morgan: no one passed along that road three days before and one day after the holdup. We'd have seen 'em."

"You don't mind if I ride that stretch of fence?"

"No, help yourself. I'm for findin' the robbers. Some of that money was mine, a good four thousand of it." He looked at Temple and squinted, forcing a myriad sea of wrinkles around his eyes. "Care to drop in for supper?"

"Not tonight, thanks."

"Nora'd be pleased with the company. She ain't

been gettin' out much since her and Miles—" He paused and studied the lighted end of his cigar. "A girl gets funny notions in her head. She gets to thinkin' that just because one man changed his mind that there must be somethin' wrong with her."

"I'll drop out to see her while I'm here," Temple promised.

The old man nodded. "Good of you, Jim. But then, you've always been a steady sort. Never seen many chips fly when you worked, but by golly the job always got done." He slapped Temple on the knee and got up carefully, mindful of his age. "I can't make up my mind about Morgan. Hate to say anything because it might be taken as a personal grudge. Nora never would tell me or her mother how far Morgan went; I've got my own ideas that it went far and she got off lucky. If I could prove it I'd kill him. But I can't prove it." He took a final puff then carefully ground out the cigar in the little hole he'd dug. "Morgan has always lived well, damned well on his salary. Maybe he had some money when he came here; I don't know. But he's a man who could stand a lot of lookin' into, Jim."

"I intend to do that. Exactly that."

Al Shannon smiled. "That satisfies me. I believe you when you say it."

He turned then, mounted his horse and rode back over the crest of the rise.

CHAPTER

FIVE

Jim Temple had his evening meal at Tom Keefer's place, and afterward they sat on the porch and drank coffee and watched the coolness of evening come across the prairie like a sigh, a relief from the long, steady heat of the day. They talked, mostly of the robbery and how it was done, then Tom announced that it was bedtime and went inside. They could hear him moving around for a time, then the house was quiet.

Near the barn, the two hired hands lived in a small building; one came out, went to the outhouse for a brief stay, then went to the well for a bucket of water, carried it back and closed the door.

"Well," Lotte said, "I hope everybody's made their nest; I thought they never would. Want to go for a walk? But take off your spurs; you sound like a bell sheep."

He laughed softly, then took off his spurs and hat and laid them on the porch railing; he took her arm and walked slowly toward the far corner of the fenced yard. They stopped near the orchard and he lifted Lotte to a perch on the fence, and she sat there, an arm gentle around his shoulders to steady herself.

She prattled on with her soft, pleasant voice and he liked it, which surprised him because he had never cared for woman talk, but he liked to listen to her. She had a quick, intelligent mind and an interest in many things; she would never become a drudge and a nag, or let the little disappointments color her life.

The jangle of a telephone broke the night silence, then a light went on in the Keefer house and a moment later Tom came out in his nightshirt and yelled in a voice loud enough to wake every sleeping thing in the country.

"Jim! OH, JIM!"

They hurried back; Keefer waited. "Damned thing, ringin' when a man's asleep." He looked at Lotte. "Ain't it past your bedtime?"

"I'm trying to get circles under my eyes," she said.

Jim Temple went down the hallway and picked up the receiver; the telephone was an oiled walnut box with an extended mouthpiece. "Temple speaking . . . yes . . . when? . . . all right . . . yes, right away." He hung up the receiver and looked at them. "Miles Morgan was found dead in his office forty minutes ago. Someone stuck a knife in him."

"Well, what do you know?" Tom Keefer said. "News like that a man ought to find out in the morning so's he can whistle all day."

"Pa!"

"Hell, I never thought anything of him when he was alive. Why should I pretend different after he's dead?"

Temple went out and braced his foot on the porch rail and put on his spurs.

"I'll get your horse," Lotte said and hurried to the barn. Keefer stood there. "How come you got your spurs off?"

"Don't you ever take your boots off?"

"Sure I do."

"Now and then I take my spurs off," Temple said.

"Are you courtin' my girl now?"

"Thinkin' about it."

"Ain't you goin' to ask my opinion?" Keefer said.

"Nope." Lotte led his horse from the barn and Temple stepped off the porch. He put a foot in the stirrup, went up, then bent low and lifted her around the waist and kissed her, her arms locked tightly around his neck.

After a moment, Keefer said, "Hey, how long does that go on anyway?"

Temple put her down gently and Lotte stepped back. "Long enough so's he'll know to come back."

Wheeling his horse, Jim Temple left the yard, trotting through the gate and not slackening his pace until he reached town. He went directly to the jail; there was a small crowd gathered outside and he pushed through, not rudely, but firmly. The constable was there, and the night deputy whom he had not yet met, a small, wrinkle-faced man with hard eyes and a shiny crown of flesh where hair had once grown. He smelled strongly of sweat and bay rum. Temple looked at him carefully, some flicker of recognition in the recesses of his mind, then he placed him, a well-known hardcase of the middle 1880's.

The constable closed the door, keeping out the curious. Miles Morgan lay on the floor, face down in a puddle of blood. The doctor was there, sitting on Morgan's desk; he was smoking a cigar and he had already made his detailed examination.

The constable said, "Looks like a jailbreak to me, Jim." He pointed toward the cell blocks where a door stood open.

Temple nodded and turned to the doctor. "Any opinion?"

"Medical. He was stabbed once, with considerable force. Not here though." He pointed back to the cells. "Back there. From the angle and position of the wound, I'd say that the man who stabbed him was lying flat on his back, in one of the cots. Morgan staggered out of the cell and back to his office. There's a few drops of blood on the floor in the corridor and both his hands are bloody, so he had obviously held the wound. He fell there, dead."

Temple looked at the deputy. "Who was in that cell?"

"Some drunks Morgan locked up personally."

"What were their names? Well, get the records, man!"

"He never booked 'em," the deputy said. He was a sullen man in his fifties, with a dense mustache and a nervous tic in his left cheek.

Temple said, "Isn't your name Hub Riley?"

"Yep."

"Then I suggest you take off that badge. You did three years for assault in 1905, and last year you were arrested on suspicion of armed robbery near Waco. That's no recommendation for being a peace officer."

"Look, mister, the mayor authorized—"

"You want me to take the badge, Riley?"

There was meanness in the man, in his eyes, in the set of his mouth, but good sense overrode this and he took off the badge, threw it on the desk and walked out.

The constable said, "I never liked him from the first."

"How long has he been here?" Temple asked.

"Oh, four and a half months, I guess. Comes on every night."

"Constable, go outside and get some men and take Morgan over to the doctor's office." He turned his head. "I suppose you'll do an autopsy, doc."

"Oh, yes. Tomorrow." He got off the desk and picked up his bag. "I'll go along. Call me if you want anything, Jim."

He stepped out as the constable came back in, closing the door and locking it. "I suspect I'd better scrub the floor before that soaks into the wood." He got a fire bucket of water and a mop and went to work. "I've been town constable for twenty years and this isn't the only mess of Morgan's I've cleaned up."

"I want to know about these three prisoners that escaped," Temple said. "Why weren't they charged or booked?"

"Don't know," the constable said, mopping furiously. "Morgan arrested 'em. Hub told me to leave 'em alone; he'd handle it." He stopped and leaned on the mop handle. "Hell, he was the deputy. What could I do, Jim?"

"But you saw 'em?"

"Well, no I didn't, Jim. You know I never hung around the jail much. My beat's always been on the street or in Judge Hanlon's courtroom. I never cottoned to Morgan so I stayed away from his stompin' ground if I could."

"But Hub saw the prisoners?"

"Oh, sure, a couple times." He watched Jim Temple. "Miles took care of 'em. I asked him if these were the same three that held up the bank." He shook his head. "They weren't. Fred Almquist came over one day, took a look, and said they wasn't. And he ought to know."

Jim Temple rolled a cigarette and thought about it, then carefully went through the pile of wanted posters, particularly the ones that had arrived in the last week.

"Did you ever hear Morgan mention any of their names?"

"Let me think."

"Why don't you go through these dodgers? Maybe it'll come to you."

"Do I have to?"

"It's part of the job," Temple said testily.

"Woody! That's it, one of 'em was called Woody. I heard Morgan call him that."

"Well, that's some help. But if they weren't charged, it can only mean they were goin' to be let out anyway, so what reason could they have had for killing Morgan? Do you suppose Morgan came across them in this stack of dodgers? You go through and see if you can find a Woody Something who's wanted."

Temple helped himself to paper and pen and wrote four pages of the report, finishing a few minutes before the constable turned over the last dodger.

"Nothin' here, Jim. No Woody."

If Temple was disappointed, he let none of it show; he sealed his letter, found stamps in the desk drawer and gave it to the constable. He tipped back Morgan's chair, the one he had sat in for so many years, and said, "Harry, I want you to send a wire to every peace officer within a radius of five hundred miles. Give them the name, Woody, and tell them to be on the lookout for three men who may be traveling together. Advise them to hold them on a blanket charge of murder. I'll wire the Rangers myself." He got up. "I'll check a bit around town and see if we can find out how they left. Either train or horses."

"They could be afoot."

"Would you be after you'd knifed a sheriff?"

"Sure wouldn't," the constable said. "I'll take care of this, Jim. You can count on me."

"Why, Harry," Temple said, a little surprised, "I always did. You're a good man; I'll ride with you any time."

Harry Randall was filled with pleasurable embarrassment; he moved his hands aimlessly a moment and smiled. "Thanks, Jim. You know, a man like me needs a kind word once in awhile, same as everybody else. Twenty years on this job, and I'm making eight dollars a month more now than when I started. That ain't much, is it? People look down on me; I know that people look down on me. Why not? When they see me coming they wonder if I've got a summons for 'em, or a notice to report for jury duty, or a complaint to serve. And I took Morgan's sass and that damned deputy he hired; all he did was bitch, lay around, or lean on the bar and drink beer. That's why I want to thank you, Jim."

He quickly shot the bolt on the door and went out.

"God damn it, he can't fire me!" Hub Riley said.

He stood in Fred Almquist's parlor, anger darkening his tan. The shades were drawn and Almquist gently puffed his cigar and watched Riley. Then he said, "Cool off. What was this job anyway? Forget it. You can take your share and get out now; you've got the best excuse a man could have."

"I think I'll stick around and see how the big Texas Ranger handles himself."

"Try and stay out of trouble," Almquist advised. "Riley, you're as clean as a new shirt. Stay that way. Morgan is dead. He was the weak one. There's nothing for the Ranger but a blind alley. Let him stumble around in it awhile."

"How about your clerk?"

"He's still in bed, hearing birdies," Almquist said. "I wouldn't be a bit surprised but what that blow on the head's knocked him so silly you wouldn't dare believe a thing he said."

"You'd better hope so."

"Hell, I know so. Of course, when he gets on his feet, I'll take him back to help me with the books. You've got to put on a show of trying, Riley. It builds public confidence. But I'm afraid Wallace isn't going to pan out. That knock will make him forgetful, unreliable, and I'll have to let him go."

He winked. "A sad thing, you know, hurt in the line of duty like that." He got up and went to the hall and looked up the stairs. "Leave by the back way and don't lock horns with Jim Temple. He'll stretch your hide on the wall to dry."

"He can't be that tough," Hub Riley said, his feelings damaged.

Almquist grinned. "Friend, I've known him for some years now and I'll tell you this about him; I've never seen a man he went after that he didn't get. He took care of Morgan's work and his own too and he never once yelled for help from anybody. Walk soft around him, Riley. It's the best advice any man could give you."

"All right, but I won't stand for him pushing me."

Almquist let him out, then lit a cigar and smoked a few minutes before leaving the house. His wife was upstairs sewing; he saw the light in her window as he went down the street. He didn't know where his daughter was; she was nineteen and it seemed to him that she was always going somewhere; he couldn't keep track of her and after awhile be simply gave up and didn't try.

Ken Wallace lived in a modest frame house on a quiet side street and Almquist went there, knocking lightly on the door. He heard movement inside, and voices, then Wallace's mother came to the door, a small, gray woman who had labored alone for fifteen years to raise a good son and never tired of talking about it.

"I'm sorry to trouble you at this hour," Almquist said in a gentle, persuasive voice, "but I thought I'd look in on Ken and see how he's getting along."

"Poorly," she said.

"Dear woman, it must be a trial for you," he said with great sympathy.

He tapped a deep well of self-pity and tears and she went on about how she had never recovered from her husband's death; she was a gusher of words, flinging them about like a handful of cast pennies. Her life had been a sorrow, a burden, and her troubles so manifold that many could not bear repeating; he listened with a mask over his boredom, his disgust; he felt sorry for the man she had married and supposed that death had been a relief from this limitless reservoir of gloom.

Yet this was what he wanted, and then he pressed two twenty-dollar bills into her moist hand; her fingers snapped over them like jaws of a trap even as her droning voice protested against her taking the money.

Finally he got to see Ken Wallace; the young man was abed, head heavily bandaged. There was a lamp by his table and when Almquist sat down, Wallace said, "I'll be as good as new in another week, sir."

"The poor boy's head is actually broken; that's what the doctor told me," Mrs. Wallace said. "He took me into his complete confidence. I insisted you know. A mother's rights. And I can be firm when I know I'm right. No mamby-pamby with me, I told him. Straight out, like a man. He saw I was strong and held nothing back. A man is nothing but jelly when faced by a determined woman."

"Mother, I'd like to talk to Mr. Almquist."

"Well, who's stopping you? I'd think you'd show more gratitude. I've waited on you hand over fist, spooned food in your mouth like a baby. It seems to me you'd give a thought to me."

Ken Wallace was embarrassed; he was a very young man, barely twenty-two, and very serious; Almquist supposed it was a defense against the endless, whining prattle and it was amazing that the boy wasn't a heavy drinker.

"Has there been anything new, sir? I mean, have the bandits been caught?"

"I'm afraid not," Almquist said. "There's a Texas Ranger here now. You know Jim Temple. Well, he's come back to take charge." He shifted in the chair. "He'll want to talk to you, Ken. I'll have him come around when you're feeling better."

"I could talk to him any time," Wallace said. "But I hardly know what to say. One minute I was standing there and the next thing I knew, I was in the doctor's office and thirty hours had just passed without me knowing it. I didn't even see what he hit me with."

"That's because you were bent over, writing."

Wallace frowned. "I don't remember that. I just never saw him." He shook his head slowly. "I just can't figure out how he got behind me, sir."

"My boy, you're confused. He was standing in front of you. Don't you remember?"

"No, sir. I don't remember that at all."

Mrs. Wallace pressed her knuckles against her mouth and stifled a sob; the tears, always ready to flow, ran down her cheeks. "Kenneth, why don't you listen to Mr. Almquist? He's trying to help you remember."

"I'm afraid I'm upsetting you both," Almquist said, rising. "I'll come back, Ken." He gave the young man a reassuring squeeze on the shoulder. "Rest, my boy. I'm sure it will all come back to you."

She showed him out, rushing on with her words, telling him how sorry she was that the boy was such a boob and that he'd come around; she'd see to that. There'd be no nonsense about it when she put her mind to it.

Almquist kept a straight face, kept his temper and his manners and left, and she turned back into the house. The hall closet door opened and Gena Almquist stepped out. The old woman tried to move past her but she put out her hand and took her by the arm, stopping her.

"Don't go back in there," she said. Her face was determined and there was a hard anger in her eyes.

"You want money, don't you? You go in there now and there won't be any more. Is that clear?"

"I'm a moth—"

"You're a selfish bitch," Gena said calmly. "Now you leave us alone." She dropped her hand and went on into the bedroom and closed the door.

Ken Wallace said, "Did he see you?"

"No, I hid in the closet. But I heard." She sat down on the edge of his bed. "Father says there were three men in the bank. Were there, Ken?"

"I didn't see them. Your father and I were going to close the door. Adam Stanton had already gone home; his wife had been sick and Mr. Almquist let him go early; it was the fourth time in a row. Not that I cared. But we were alone. I'll swear that, Gena."

"And he swears there were three men. Others saw them around town too." She bent forward and looked closely at him. "I love you, Ken, but we've got to get it straight. Father says you can't remember. Wouldn't it be if you've forgotten this, then you've forgotten other things?"

"I—I'd think so."

"All right, let's find out? When's your birthday?"

"April 9."

"What kind of a day was it when the bank was robbed?"

"It started off a little cloudy. When I was walking up town I passed Llano Stiles sweeping

92

off the walk in front of the saloon and he remarked to me that it was possible we'd get a little sprinkle to settle the dust."

"What time was that?"

"A quarter to eight."

"What were you wearing?"

"My light fawn suit." He smiled. "And that nice tie you gave me for my birthday."

"After you'd been hit on the head and woke up in the doctor's office, what's the first thing you remember?"

"The doc said, 'Had enough sleep, Ken?'"

"Who was there?"

"The sheriff and the doc and the constable. I didn't see the deputy, Hub Riley. It was dark, quite late. I could see the wall clock without turning my head and it was a quarter after ten. I knew it had to be at night because I'd been in the bank at four so—"

"You remember fine," Gena said, smiling. "Now, what were you doing when the lights went out?"

"I was just about through adding the day's receipts," he said. "There was an interest error in one of the accounts and I'd found it and everything balanced nicely. Just a split second before I was hit I glanced at Mr. Almquist; he was alone at his desk behind the wicket. Then, pow!" He shook his head. "He and I were alone when I got hit. All except for the man that hit me. He must have used a piece of lead pipe. I just recall a peculiar odor, then I got hit on the head."

She sat a moment, her hands gentle on him. "Ken, why is my father lying?"

"I didn't say that he was. Gena, maybe I don't remember it all."

"There's nothing wrong with your memory, Ken. Where were the three men when this happened? Why does he say there were three men when there weren't?"

"Honey, I just don't know." He patted her hand. "It's late. You'd better get home."

"Father won't really miss me," she said. "Ken, you're not going back to the bank, are you?"

"What else is there?"

"Leave here. Go somewhere else."

He frowned. "And leave my mother?"

"It would be the best thing that ever happened to her," Gena said. "She'd have the rest of her life to tell everyone what an unfaithful son you were, and she'd be very happy with all that misery to spread."

"Gena, how can you say that?"

"Because it's true," she told him. "Not pretty, but true. We have to face things, Ken. Neither of us could face out my father and tell him that we wanted to get married. We just don't have that kind of courage; and that's not an easy truth to face. Some people can do brave, noble things, but we can't, Ken. We have to sneak around and meet where no one will see us, or here where your mother is afraid to talk for fear of killing the golden goose."

"You've given her money again."

"Yes."

He shook his head. "I don't know which is worse, you giving it to her or her taking it. Don't any of us have any pride, Gena? God, I wish I had it. I wish I could stand straight and look at a man and tell him to go to the devil because it was the right thing to do. But I can't. I'll smile and choke it back and hate myself for it afterward." He stopped talking a moment as though flooded by unpleasant things. "It hurts when a man will say, 'Hey, boy, come over here!' I want to look him in the eye and tell him my name is Mr. Wallace and if he wants to talk to me to show a little respect. Then I think of your father and my job and mother whining and I choke it all back and say 'yes, sir.' If I was a man, a real man, I'd take you somewhere else and never give it a thought. But I'm not and I just can't do it."

"You will, Ken. I know you will."

"Why do you have faith in me?"

"Because I love you and I think I see a part of you that you don't even know exists."

He sighed. "I hope to God it does exist. I don't want to disappoint you, Gena."

CHAPTER

SIX

Jim Temple asked questions. He wrote the answers down and after a day of this he began to come up with some contradictions. Nothing big, but little contradictions, things that just didn't come out the same when he figured they should have.

He went to Ken Wallace's house and talked with the mother, and then he talked with Wallace, all the time writing it down, and that night he worked until nearly midnight, setting all the information straight, and writing another report—ten pages this time—to Captain Rickert.

The next day he went to Fred Almquist's house and his daughter answered the door; she said that her father had gone fishing and after getting the general direction, Jim Temple rode along the river for better than a mile before he found Almquist; he was sitting under a tree, his pole propped on a small rock and weighed down with another.

"Expect to catch anything?" Temple asked. He dismounted and tied his horse.

"No. And I didn't expect to be bothered either."

"Into each life a little rain must fall." Temple sat

down and stretched his long legs. "I'd like to talk to you about those three men who held you up, Fred. The constable tells me you came over to the jail once and took a look at 'em."

"That's right. What of it?"

"He said you couldn't identify 'em."

"So?"

"So it brings up a question or two that needs answerin'," Temple said. "Now I guess I've talked to just about everyone in town and the bartender over at The Saddleman's told me he'd gone over to the jail one night to bring Morgan sandwiches and beer, and he recognized the three men as the ones who came into his place and went out the back way."

"What's that supposed to prove anyway?"

Temple shrugged. "Oh, I suppose not much, but it could mean that those three Morgan had in lock-up weren't the ones who held you up so I thought I'd better ask you for sure whether or not you made a positive identification."

Almquist frowned and pushed his tongue around in his cheek a moment. "You put me in an embarrassing position, Jim. Damned embarrassing."

"How's that?"

"Well, several things there. First off, I haven't let on this to anyone, but I was scared. When I looked up, Wallace was falling; that was the first inkling I had that anything was wrong. The truth of it is, I'm not a brave man. Not brave at all. Oh, I talk big, but it's bluff, Jim. Pure bluff. Was I ever called, I'd fold. That's the way I am." He kept looking down at his knees while he talked and his voice got little, as though he were too ashamed to speak up or look up. "I never really got a good look at the bandits, Jim. Wallace was hit on the head and—and I fainted."

"Oh, for Christ's sake!" Temple let the disgust rush out before he could think to check it and he was sorry, but it was done and he couldn't take it back.

"Yes," Almquist said softly. "It's the way anyone would react. But you have to be afraid all the time to know what it's like." He forced himself to look at Temple. "To cover it up, I—I made up the descriptions. They'd fit most any average man. What could I do, Jim? I'd lost everything. Did I have to lose what little self-respect I had left?"

"I guess not. What about your identification at the jail?"

Almquist said, "Jim, it was night and the light was poor and I just pretended to glance at them. It was a lie too."

"But you said—"

"For God's sake, man, spare me something!" He calmed himself with considerable effort. "I said they weren't the ones because I was afraid they were and if they got out they'd come for me and kill me."

Jim Temple sighed and dug dirt from the river bank and let it sift through his fingers. "Then they could well have been the ones. It kind of figures that maybe Morgan stumbled onto something and they killed him and made a get-away. Well, it's a theory. The best we have to date." He got up as though to leave. "Oh, one more thing, Fred; I had a long talk with Ken Wallace. He doesn't remember any men being in the bank at all."

"The boy's had a terrible knock. It's surprising he knows his own mother."

"Maybe. The doctor wouldn't say one way or another; they're a cagey lot."

"They could have killed the boy," Almquist said. "It makes me sick to think of it, a nice fella like Ken, addled because of one man's brutality."

"Yeah, it's too bad." He smiled. "Fred, we're all different. Try and remember that."

"Little consolation there."

"We're all different and we all have our part of living."

"Jim, you're not going to say—"

"No, no, this is between ourselves."

He got his horse and rode out and Fred Almquist watched him go, then he pared the wrapper from a cigar, lit it, and let his smile broaden until laughter bubbled from him. After he had enjoyed his joke he said, "Almquist, you should have been on the stage."

● ● ●

Jim Temple spent the next two days sitting on the hotel porch where the shade was good; he tipped his chair back and elevated his feet and sat there. He had a table brought out, and now and then he sent someone for a glass of beer and ate his noonday meal there and hardly spoke to anyone at all.

Most everyone saw him sitting there and wondered about it, but no one asked him why. Miles Morgan's funeral drew a good crowd, but Temple did not go and this started a little talk because Temple had worked for Morgan for quite a few years and it hardly seemed gracious.

Then the telegrapher sent his messenger boy to the hotel with a telegram for Jim Temple, and an hour later the Ranger was at the depot, buying his ticket for El Paso. Harry Randall, the constable, whose curiosity was more official than anyone else's, came to the station and found Temple waiting on the platform for his train to arrive. There was a fair crowd at the station and Randall spoke so that no one else could hear.

"You just ain't—ah—you're comin' back, ain't you?"

"I'll be back," Temple said. "I don't want it to get around town at all—that's why I cautioned the telegrapher to keep his mouth shut—but the marshal in El Paso picked up our three flown birds."

"Well, I'll be damned!"

"He's holdin' 'em for me. I should be back in a week."

"I'll keep this to myself," Randall promised, and meant it.

"Harry, you could do somethin' for me while I'm gone. Keep a pretty close eye on Ken Wallace's house for me."

"What am I watchin' for?"

"Who comes and goes. Anything. Take care that you're not obvious about it."

Randall winked. "Consider it done, Jim."

Temple had to change trains in Roswell, New Mexico, and there was a brief layover, enough time for him to get a haircut, a shave, and a bath. When he arrived in El Paso, a policeman outside the station gave him directions to the city jail; he presented his credentials to the sergeant and was turned over to a captain, a gruff-voiced man in a tight suit.

"Sergeant, you're welcome to 'em," the captain said, waving his hands. "Never mind papers. I'll turn 'em over to you and be happy to do it."

"Real hard cases, huh?"

The captain stared. "Hell, no, nothing like that. They sing."

"They what?"

"Harmonize. All the time. Day and night. Must know a hundred songs." He put his hands to his head and rocked it back and forth. "No one's had a decent night's sleep for two nights."

"That sure is strange," Temple admitted.

"They're brothers, you know."

"No, I didn't know."

"Their name is Adams. Woody, Otis, and Marv." He shook his head. "Murder? It's hard to believe. A patrolman on South El Paso Street saw them and phoned in to check. They were in one of the Mexican bars, singing for drinks and not a dime between them. Submitted to arrest with no fuss at all. Armed too." He threw out his hands. "They're yours, sergeant, and I hope you have an ear for music."

"Sing off key, huh?"

"No," he said, letting his voice swoop up on the vowel. "They sing right well. But a steady diet—" He shook his head again.

"Well, I'm going to take 'em back," Temple said. "You wouldn't happen to have a railroad schedule handy, would you?"

The captain had one in his desk. "The next northbound is late tomorrow afternoon. If you're in a hurry, I'd say your best bet was to take the train to Midlands. They've got some bridge trouble across the Pecos, but I reckon they have it fixed by now. You could catch that train in two hours."

"That's fine," Temple said. "Since I'm only covered with a John Doe warrant, I'd just as soon keep them in the State of Texas. Could I see 'em now?"

"Sure, I'll have 'em brought over." He turned to a wall phone and cranked it furiously, contacted the head jailer, then hung up. "Be ten minutes or so. Care for some coffee? They always have some in the squad room down the hall."

"Sounds fine." He left the office with the captain and they went into the squad room, a long corridor flanked by lockers and split down the middle by wooden tables shoved end to end. There were at least a dozen policemen in the room, some playing cards, some dressing for a tour of duty.

They started to come to attention when the captain stepped in but he waved his hand and they relaxed. "Gentlemen, this is Sergeant Jim Temple, Company E, Texas Rangers. He's come to take the songbirds off our hands."

They cheered him and he laughed and took a cup of coffee that was offered. One of the policemen said, "Sergeant, the patrolman who made the arrest is in my squad and he tells me the Adams boys were pretty surprised when they found they were being held for murder."

"They claim to know nothing about it," the captain said.

"Did they admit being in Tascosa?"

"Yes. Admitted to spending some time in jail too. The sheriff there locked them up for having

103

no visible means of support." He pawed his face out of shape. "They tell a pretty straightforward story, sergeant. But, the best liars are always the most convincing ones. Now you take a man who's innocent and is being arrested for the first time in his life. He's nervous. He sweats. He forgets or contradicts himself. If you looked at him and judged him, you'd take him right out and hang him then and there. But I was on the force when John Selman killed Wes Hardin. Knew Hardin slightly. A very cool customer. He could look you in the eye and smile and lie his way out of most anything. The only difference between the Adams boys and Hardin is that Hardin didn't sing." He nodded toward Temple's coffee. "If you're about finished with that, we'll go back. The paddy wagon ought to be showing up."

Temple drank what was left of his coffee and put the cup on the table. "Nice to have met you fellas," he said and went out with the captain.

The wagon had arrived and the Adams brothers were in the hall, handcuffed; the captain waved them inside and the two officers stood outside by the closed door.

They were young men; the oldest was near thirty, all tall men, dressed in badly worn clothing. Yet Temple noticed that their faces and hands were clean and they stood together, straight and not afraid at all.

"This is Sergeant Jim Temple, Texas Rangers. He's come to take you bye-bye."

They knew this without being told and they watched Temple coolly. He said, "We're going back to Tascosa. We're going to take the train. Now I'll tell you how it's going to be. I'm going to take the handcuffs off and you can ride like ordinary men. Or you can make one move to escape and finish the journey in the baggage car —dead!" It got to them, this plain talk. "I don't shoot to wound. I'll shoot to kill and it won't take much to get me started bangin' away. Now if you think it's brag or bluff, it'll cost you a dead man to find out." He looked from one to the other, then settled on the oldest. "What's your name?"

"Woodrow. Call me Woody."

"What about it, Woody?"

He scratched his beard stubble. "Well, I sure didn't kill anybody so I guess I'll just sit quietly and let the judge turn me loose proper."

Temple switched his eyes to the middle one, and the man said, "I'm Otis. I didn't kill nobody either, so I'll ride without fuss."

"You?" Temple asked, looking at the youngest.

"I'm Marv. I got no reason to be jumpy, and less to be dead."

The captain frowned. "Sergeant, I don't want to seem to be telling you your business, but aren't you taking hell of a chance?"

"No, they are," Temple said calmly. "The first

one that tries to get up out of his seat without asking first will never remember falling back into it." Without warning, he suddenly popped his .44 free and showed them what the muzzle looked like. "You see?"

Woody Adams swallowed hard and looked at his brothers. "Sure as hell do," he said quietly. "Yes, sir!"

Checking them out of the El Paso jail was no problem; Temple signed for their personal effects after they were counted and listed in front of witnesses, then these were placed in a box and sealed to be mailed later in the day.

A patrol wagon took them to the depot and Temple insisted on riding in back with the prisoners. At the station he got down and the Adams brothers stood together; the sergeant and driver pulled away and Temple herded them into the station and they waited by the wicket while he got the tickets, paying for them with a chit drawn against the Texas Ranger budget.

He wasn't much for talk, herding them over to benches with a nod of the head. There was a lot of traffic in the depot; it was a large building, full of noise and hurry; they sat down to wait for train time.

Finally Woody Adams said, "Sergeant, who is it we're supposed to have killed anyway?"

"You tell me," Temple said.

"I can't 'cause we didn't kill anybody."

"Try the sheriff, Miles Morgan."

They showed a genuine surprise. "Aw, hell, sergeant, he let us out of jail so we could catch the ten o'clock freight. Is he dead?"

"And buried. Your cell door was open. Looks bad, doesn't it?"

"That's a fact," Woody said, genuinely worried now. "He let us out, sergeant. We didn't break out."

"Well boys, you were in jail and you got out and the sheriff's dead and there's no record of you being released."

"No record of us being arrested either," Otis pointed out.

"It's up to the court, not me," Temple said and lapsed into silence. The caller came through, announcing their train, and Temple motioned for them to get up and get outside. They waited on the platform while the train was loading, then got on as nearly last as they could, taking seats in the chair car near the smoking car.

For better than two hours they rocked and bolted along and no one said anything, then Jim Temple shattered the silence. "I hear you fellas are some singers. You lose your voice?"

"Don't feel like it now," Marv Adams said. "You feel like it, Otis? Woody?"

They shook their heads. Woody said, "I can't get over it, the sheriff dead. He was such a nice fella too. Gave us two dollars apiece when he let us out of jail."

"All right now," Temple said, out of patience. "I know Miles Morgan and he wouldn't give a dime to see the Statue of Liberty do an about face. What are you tryin' to hand me anyway?"

"It's the truth," Otis said. "Swear to God. He gave us each two dollars and hoped our luck would pick up."

They all nodded, and Jim Temple studied them, studied their faces, their eyes; they were the most sincere-looking men he'd ever seen, and he would have sworn that they had been raised by strict parents who pounded them raw for lying.

"All right, I'm going to ask questions. I'm going to ask 'em fast and I want answers fast. And no one of you does the talking. No one answers two questions in a row. Understand?"

"Yes, sir," Woody said, nodding.

"Where you from?"

"Paris, Texas," Woody said.

"What county?"

"Lamar," Otis replied.

"Parents live there?"

"Both dead," Marv said.

"How did you get into Tascosa?"

"Late freight," Woody said. "We took that freight because some hobo said the yard bulls were rough on that line."

"Where did you sleep that night?"

"Behind the saloon." Marv said.

"What gave you the idea to rob the bank?"

"We didn't rob any bank," Woody said. "We've never stole anything, sergeant."

"Did once," Otis said. "Remember that apple orchard—"

"That ain't real stealin', a few apples," Woody said.

"You're all lyin'," Temple said harshly. "You robbed the bank."

"Not lyin' and didn't rob the bank," Otis insisted.

"Less than twenty minutes after the bank was robbed you went into the saloon. What did you do?"

"Got some free lunch and went out the back way," Woody said. "Otis thought he'd lost a sack of tobacco there."

"How did you get out of town?"

"We didn't," Woody said. "The sheriff came down the alley, asked us what the hell we were lookin' for, then took us to the jailhouse. He locked us up, gave us a sack of tobacco and a pail of water. There was a hell of a hubbub goin' on in town, so we figured we was best out of it."

"The sheriff came in with a sack of grub, then locked the jail tight as a drum," Otis said. "Sounded like he was gettin' up a posse. Leastways a hell of a lot of horsemen left town. So we minded what we was told, kept our mouth shut and waited until he came back. That was two days later."

"Little more than that," Marv said. "He left in the evenin' and didn't get back until—"

"All right, all right," Temple said, drawing them silent. "Are you settin' there, tellin' me that Morgan was out chasin' you when he had you in jail?"

"He couldn't be chasin' us," Woody said. "We hadn't done anything at all."

"All right, let me ask one thing more. The captain in El Paso said you sang all the time. How come you didn't do any singin' in the Tascosa jail?"

"The sheriff told us we could have room and board as long as we kept our mouths shut," Otis said. He rolled his shoulders slightly and shook his head once. "Now I wouldn't say it made sense to us at the time, but the place was clean and the meals were good. The day after the sheriff came back from all his runnin' around, he told us we could stay a week or so if we did what he said."

"What did he say?"

"Kind of funny," Woody said. "He wanted us to make out we'd just been locked up. What the hell, like Otis says, the food was good and we weren't headin' anywhere in particular anyway."

"Wasn't there anyone else in jail besides you three?"

"Well, there was some cowboys that'd been whoopin' it up," Marv said, "but the sheriff always kept them way up front. We had a cell in the back, near the storeroom."

"Who did you see when you were there?"

"The deputy," Woody said. "That's all. There was another lawman who'd drop in once in awhile, we could hear him talkin'. Kind of high voice. But he never once came back into the cell block where we was."

"How come you were in El Paso?"

"Just couldn't get work," Marv said. "This time of the year, no one's puttin' on hands, and ranchin' is all we know. We thought we'd sign up for a hitch in the cavalry at Fort Bliss. Twenty-one dollars a month, food, and found. It could tide a man over."

"Between the three of us we figured to save a thousand dollars in three years," Otis said. "We ain't much for cards and we don't booze it up like some do."

Jim Temple studied them for several minutes. "Now there's one of two things here. You're either three of the smoothest liars I've ever met, or someone's been lyin' right down the line and it ain't you."

"It ain't us," Woody said. "Loafin' we're good at. Bummin' a meal—I'd say average."

"Maybe a little better," Otis put in.

"I guess there's no sense in bein' modest," Woody admitted. "We're better than average. But lyin' we don't do worth a damn."

"Very poorly," Marv added. He sat back and crossed his arms. "So, we didn't rob anybody or kill anybody and you can peck at us a hunnert years and we won't change our story none. One thing about stickin' to the truth; you don't have to remember what you said." He nudged Otis. "How about a song?" He hummed a few bars. "That about the right key?"

"Suits me. Whatcha singin'?"

"How about 'Tentin' Tonight'?"

" 'Old Rugged Cross'," Woody said. "I'm in the mood."

"That's a goodie," Marv said and established the pitch.

They had clear, resonant voices, and a fine ear for harmony and they were not through the verse when people began to leave their seats and gather at that end of the coach. Temple speculated on whether or not he should stop it; they could make a break in a crowd and he'd be helpless, then he decided to chance it.

Let them have rope, if they wanted that.

The second verse reduced a drygoods drummer to damp eyes and he offered them a dollar to sing 'Abide With Me.'

Woody Adams glanced at Temple and said, "Can we take it?"

"Sure."

"What's he got to say about it?" the drummer asked.

"He's a good man," Otis said and then began to sing.

CHAPTER
SEVEN

By laying over and changing trains at Midland, Jim Temple arrived at the jail with his prisoners a little before midnight; Harry Randall was sleeping in the office and he woke up and locked the Adams boys in a cell while Temple washed up in the sheriff's office.

The constable came back and hung up the large ring of keys. "They won't break out this time," he said and ran his fingers through his rumpled hair.

"I'm not so sure they broke out before," Temple said. "I particularly noticed that the keys were not near Morgan's body. Did you pick them off the floor and hang them up, Harry?"

"No. Everything was exactly as you found it."

Temple nodded and walked over to the spare bunk. "Without further ado, I bid you good night. I've had damned little sleep the last two and a half days. I'll book them in the morning after I've had a talk with Almquist and the city attorney." He removed his boots and gunbelt and settled back, closing his eyes and a few minutes later he was gently snoring.

Around eight, Randall woke him when he

accidentally slammed the front door; he was coming in with a tray of food for the prisoners and was closing the door with his foot when it got away from him and closed suddenly. Temple yawned and stretched and tugged on his boots, then went out to find an early-opening barbershop and a shave. He ate in a restaurant then went back to the jail for awhile; there was no point in interrupting the county attorney's breakfast.

He walked back to the cell block; the Adams brothers were sitting there, smoking, and being very quiet. "You'll be charged today," Jim Temple said.

Woody looked up. "You don't believe us."

"Fella, it's not what I believe. The court's got to have its say. Better that way. If you're cleared, the law is through botherin' you."

"And if we ain't?" Otis asked.

Temple raised his eyebrows and blew out his breath. "Let's worry about that when we come to it, huh?"

He decided he had waited long enough and left the jail, walking west until he came to Lyle Pollack's house. His wife let Temple in; Pollack was just finished with his second cup of coffee and he invited Temple to pull up a chair.

"Heard you were out of town, Jim. Sit down."

"Thanks," Temple said, scraping back a chair. "Lyle, I brought back the three men Miles Morgan had in jail. They were arrested in El Paso; I went there and got 'em."

114

"Alone? That wasn't too smart. I mean, they could have jumped you and—"

"They didn't do that. Lyle, I think we'd better talk this over with Fred Almquist and either charge these men or let them go."

"Let them go?" Pollack frowned and smiled at the same time. "Jim, we've got a case here."

"How do you know? You haven't heard their testimony yet."

"I'll call Fred," Pollack said and went to the hall and telephoned. Pollack's wife, a plump, smiling woman whose sole occupation was cooking and endless child-bearing, filled Temple's coffee cup. The children came whooping into the kitchen, seven of them; they lined up for clean face inspection, pats, kisses, lunch boxes, then stormed out of the house with a thumping of feet and banging of doors, racing for the schoolhouse and the warning bell's urging peal.

"Schools were invented by mothers who couldn't stand it all day," she said and turned to a mountain of washing on the back porch.

Pollack came back. "Fred will meet us at his house in twenty minutes. This is very good news, Jim, but I hope we can keep the citizens quiet. After all, they lost a lot of money and the town is without a bank." He pursed his lips and tapped his cheek with his finger. "The question that comes to my mind is who we're going to get to defend them. It won't be a popular case, you know. Not saying that Morgan was well loved, but he was popular with many; most easygoing men are."

"Lyle, wouldn't you like to hear their statement?"

"Time for that," he said, waving his hand. "Plenty of time. I want to prepare a good case, Jim. Naturally I'll expect your help."

"I'll provide what evidence I can dig up," Temple assured him, "but I wouldn't want to manufacture any."

Pollack stared at him. "What a thing to say! I never asked you to do that. Yes, I want a conviction. It's going to be a big case. A man's future is made on such cases. But I'm for a fair trial."

"Good to hear you say that," Temple murmured, and Pollack missed the sarcasm.

"While you were gone," Pollack said, "the supervisors met and appointed Hub Riley to fill out Morgan's term of office."

"You're jokin'!"

"No, there really wasn't anyone else," Pollack insisted. "It took some persuasion, but in the end we were all convinced that Hub was the man for the job."

"Convinced by whom?"

"Well, Fred Almquist mostly. Why not? The man's mayor, a civic leader. He's given us good advice before."

"Not this time, Lyle." Temple drank his coffee and got up. "Let's go, huh?"

• • •

Fred Almquist met them on his porch, all smiles and handshakes; they went into the parlor and he closed the large walnut doors leading to the hall and then poured three whiskey glasses. "Gentlemen," he said expansively, "may I offer a toast to the Texas Rangers, who always get their man. Men in this case." He raised his glass and Pollack tossed his off. Then they looked at Temple. "Aren't you going to drink to that, Jim?" Almquist asked.

"I'd just as soon we cut out this all-for-the-regiment bullshit and got down to business," Jim Temple said, bringing out his notebook. They looked at him, a bit stunned, a little hurt, and some surprised, then they took chairs. "Now the way I've got this sized up can be put into one word: trouble. First off, any lawyer defending them would put them on the stand to testify and if he did that, you'd end up with a pretty thin case of circumstantial evidence."

Pollack bristled; he was like many attorneys who feel that only they are entitled to an opinion. "Suppose you permit me to weigh the evidence, Jim. I'll decide how to handle the case."

"Why, that was my intention all along," Temple said and began to read from his notebook. He built frowns on their faces and glances between them and when he closed his notebook, they sat there and looked at him.

"Do you mean to tell me," Almquist asked, "that these men have the gall to insist that they are innocent?"

"Yep. All the way around." He dropped it into Almquist's lap. "You never did make a positive identification, Fred. We're going to have to have more than we have to take this to the grand jury for an indictment."

Lyle Pollack spread his hands. "The solution is obvious. Fred, you go to the jail and make a positive identification." He scrubbed his hands together as though he were about to be awarded a grand prize and could hardly wait to get it. "Jim, I would say that your work has been well done. Wouldn't you say that, Fred?"

"I certainly would. And I'm going to write a glowing letter to your captain about your efficiency."

"Oh, he'll think that's keen," Temple said.

Almquist frowned slightly. "You'll go far, Jim; I always said that. But now it's up to the legal wheels to turn." He got up and took Temple gently by the elbow. "So if you'll let us get at it, let us get our heads together—" He kept steering Temple toward the door, and into the hallway and outside on the porch, talking all the while. "—a shining example of law enforcement, Jim: that's what I call it. I'll get that letter off this evening. What was his name again? Rickert?"

"You have a fine memory," Jim Temple said

and walked back toward the main street.

Fred Almquist watched him go, smiling, waving, and when Temple passed out of sight, he let his smile quickly fade and turned to go back inside, stopping when he saw his daughter leaning against the door frame.

"Why didn't you kiss him, daddy?"

"Your smart mouth can get you in a lot of trouble," Almquist snapped. "And where the devil were you at eleven o'clock last night?"

"Out."

"I know you were out. Do you think I'm an idiot?"

She smiled sweetly. "I think there's some things parents shouldn't discuss with their children. And the other way around." She turned with a swirl of skirt and bounce of braided hair and retreated into the house, leaving him with his concern and his anger and his frustration.

He went back into the parlor where Lyle Pollack was helping himself to one of Almquist's cigars. "Why don't you take a couple for later?"

"Why, thank you," Pollack said and put four in his coat pocket. "Fred, I think—"

"Please," Almquist said, holding up his hand and closing his eyes. "Let's not indulge ourselves in fantasy. The only answer, as I see it, is a full confession from the three men." He put his hands behind him and paced back and forth for a moment. "Lyle, I know you have political ambitions, and you know that I'm for you one hundred per cent. This is an opportunity of a lifetime for you."

"Yes, Fred, I realize it."

"You don't quite understand me," Almquist said. "We have a tough one to crack here, three stubborn men who deny any connection with the robbery or the murder. If you prosecuted and failed to wring a confession from them, if you made a mess of it and there was an acquittal, or a mistrial, you couldn't run for county office again with a hope of winning." He tapped his cheek with his finger. "I've been thinking of someone else, Lyle, someone who is known throughout the state, someone important. You would assist him, brilliantly of course, and your future would be more secure."

"Who?"

"State Senator Lon Barrett." He watched Pollack carefully. "The legislature is not in session. Why not? Lon and I are old friends. I've made some bountiful contributions to his campaigns. As a matter of fact, I've been thinking of opening a bank in Webb County. Lon is a formidable public speaker; he could sway a deaf jury with his courtroom manner. Can't you see this, Lyle, three itinerant cowboys pitted against one of the finest legal minds in Texas? Why, they wouldn't have a chance. He'd have them crossed up, caught in their own lies before they knew what happened. And he'd get a conviction on that, even if he didn't get a confession from them. A conviction is what we want, Lyle. You need it. We all need it. Justice must be satisfied."

"I'd been going along with the idea of handling this myself, Fred."

"It's too big for you. Face it. Do it my way and you may sit in the state legislature someday." He came over and put his arm around Pollack's shoulders and gave him an affectionate squeeze. "My boy—may I call you my boy? I've watched you these years, studying law at night—a young Abe Lincoln all over again, working tirelessly to pass your bar examinations. I've watched you campaign, listened to you speak, observed that homespun honesty and looked into your unsullied face, unmarked by graft and money under the table. I respect you, Lyle. I want to help you. Accept an older, wiser man's advice now."

"This is all very touching, Fred. Very touching."

"Nonsense. I want you to have the best, Lyle, because you're a sincere man, and I admire and respect a sincere man." He clapped Pollack on the shoulder. "Let's go over to the jail; I want to take a look at these three hoodlums. And I want to call the newspaper editor. I'll get my hat."

Almquist made his phone call, then walked with Pollack to the jail. The newspaper man, whose office was just down the street from the jail, was already there. Hub Riley sat behind Morgan's desk and Jim Temple lounged against the wall.

Riley took them back, all except Temple, who didn't see any point in going. He remained against the wall; he could hear everything that was said.

Fred Almquist looked a long moment at the Adams brothers, then said, "Yes. I can say positively that these are the men who held up my bank."

Woody said, "What are you saying, mister? We've never seen you before."

"You're the one who hit my teller," Almquist said. He turned and came back to the office, glanced at Temple, then stepped outside and waited for Lyle Pollack and the newspaper editor to join him. He said, "I've never been more positive; you can quote me on that. And we all hope and pray that when young Wallace is confronted with them, his memory will return and he'll be in good health again. Good day, gentlemen."

Hub Riley came back, hung up the keys and toed the door closed. He looked at Jim Temple. "Is there any reason you have to hang around my office?"

There were a lot of things about this man that Temple could easily take offense at, but he kept the feeling under control. "You take good care of the prisoners, huh?"

"Now I sure will do that. Don't hurry back."

"If I have to come back, I will," Temple assured him and went out.

He stopped in one of the saloons and bought a pitcher of beer and took it to his room; he had a very long report to write and he found it difficult to stick to the facts because his opinions kept cropping up and he kept pushing them down, knowing good and well that Captain George Rickert didn't give a damn for an opinion.

The envelope was bulky when he sealed it; he took it to the post office, bought a stamp and dropped it in the mail slot, then got on his horse and rode out to Tom Keefer's place, feeling very depressed.

Lotte was washing and hanging clothes and Tom and his two hired hands were cultivating a field in the south corner of the place; Temple knew that he wouldn't come in until noon; farmers were that way, not interrupting their chores unless the barn caught fire or one of the kids fell down the well.

Temple took his horse to the barn and unsaddled; he left his pistol belt there, and walked toward the house. Lotte had a basket full of wet clothes and a bag of clothespins tied around her waist; he carried the basket, moving slowly along with her while she hung the clothes. The heat was fierce and sweat soaked her cotton blouse, making it cling to her shoulders and back; she didn't talk because she kept her mouth full of clothespins, as though they were wooden cigars.

Finally she reached the bottom of the basket and got rid of the clothespins. "You're pretty husky for a growing boy," she said, smiling impishly. "Want a steady job?"

"How's the pay?"

"Poor, but the meals are good and the evenings will be interesting."

"I think the offer has some merit," Temple admitted. "Don't you get tired of working so hard?"

"Sure, then I get tired of everything getting dirty again. Some choice, huh? You're tired from cleaning everything, or tired of seeing everything dirty. There's just no winning." She walked to the back step and sat down, planking herself, stretching out her legs. There was a cotton towel hanging on the railing and she wiped sweat from her face and pushed back her hair. Then she sniffed the towel and tossed it in the washtub. "Sour. Everything turns sour in this heat." She tipped her head back and squinted at the sky. There was no breath of air; the land seemed to be gripped in a hush and to the northeast the sky turned murky, quite dark near the horizon. "I think it's building up for a gully-buster. Should be getting wind soon. I keep watching for dust devils."

He took out his sack tobacco and started to make a cigaret but she took paper and tobacco from him and said, "Let me." She crimped the paper, poured, shook it even, then rolled it with one hand and laughed as she licked it. "Ain't that clever?"

"You're some kid." He took the smoke and scratched a match on the edge of the porch step. "I guess you heard I was out of town." She nodded. "I brought back the three men that were seen right after the holdup. There's some suspicion that they may have done in Morgan, but I really don't think so. Fact is, I don't think they robbed the bank at all, although Almquist swears they're the same men."

"So what do you do about it?"

"The law's like machinery; it's got to turn over before it accomplishes anything. I figure it's best if they're charged, tried, and freed. That way it won't be hangin' over their heads." He looked at his hands a moment. "What I came out here for was to ask your pa if he could help me get a lawyer for the fellas. They don't have a dime and if the court appoints one it'll be some muckle-head from Ady or Vega who'll make a half-hearted defense just because he's been told to. On my pay I couldn't afford a thing, but I've got some savings I'd throw in and I'd—"

"When pa comes in this noon, you talk to him," Lotte said. "I think he'd want to do something, Jim. There are others that would too if it meant pinnin' something on Almquist." He looked at her oddly. "I guess you haven't been out to Spur and talked to Carlos Rameras."

"No. There wasn't any reason to."

"Now you've got a reason," she said and got up.

"Come on, I'll fix you some cold tea." She took him by the hand and he went into the kitchen with her. Surprisingly, the thick adobe kept out the heat and she got an ice pick from the sink drawer, opened a trapdoor in the floor and went down into the cool depths of the icehouse. The walls were stone and the ice, cut during the winter from the creek, was covered with thick sawdust; she dragged out a piece with tongs, chipped some into a wooden pail and brought it up to be washed.

"I didn't know Tom had an icehouse."

"Used to be a root cellar," she said. A breeze husked across the yard, lifting a swirl of dust and teasing the shade trees. It boomed in through the open window, a gust of it, strong and cool and full of the promise of weather. "There'll be mud tonight. Well, the creek's getting low anyway." The windmill began to creak and thump, picking up speed and she said, "I'd better go shut that—"

"I'll do it," he said and went out. The sky to the northeast was black and he knew that a storm was on the way. The wind was a power and the windmill ran even faster. He climbed the ladder, wrestled with the vane and finally cocked it over and locked it there and the blades slowly died; the pump stopped spewing water into the cattle tank.

As he came down, Tom and the hands came in with the team and cultivator; the hands took the team to the barn and Tom went to the house. "She'll lift shingles tonight," he said and washed his face at the stand. The clothes Lotte had hung out were flailing at a good angle to the line, but there was no danger yet of their blowing away.

They went into the house and the hands came in from the barn, washed and slicked down their hair, then came in and sat down at the table. Lotte was putting out the glasses of iced tea and the two hired hands smiled their thanks. They were men in their fifties and had worked steadily for Tom Keefer for many years.

Jim Temple said, "Can I ask you a personal question, Tom?"

"Sure. I may not answer, but you can sure ask it."

Lotte was at the stove, cooking and Keefer leaned his elbows on the table and waited for Temple to speak. "It ain't much of a secret, Tom, but what folks consider you the most successful farmer in the county."

"That be the plain truth," Keefer said with no modesty at all.

"How do you do it?"

"I take the trouble," Keefer said. He leaned back and smiled. "First off, all these farmers, except me, raise mainly one thing year after year. Olson raises sugar beets. Not much else. I don't do that. I've got a whole section here, and there never once was more than two thirds of it planted at one time. And I never plant the same crop two years runnin' on the same piece of land. Hell, it makes sense, don't it? You take a man for example. He's awake maybe eighteen hours out of twenty-four, then he's got to sleep. Land is the same way, Jim. It's got to rest. My land rests one year out of three. The same applies to plantin' the same crops. Suppose you had to saw wood. Your arms and back would get tired, wouldn't they? Crops are the same. Different things take certain things out of the soil."

"Those are mighty peculiar notions," Jim Temple said.

"Maybe, but I cut hay four times to everyone's three," Keefer said. "I hand-feed cattle, beef and dairy. I've got hogs, sheep, and eight head of horses. I've got a brooder house with poultry, and it all keeps me hoppin', but at the end of the year I'm not cryin' because the sun cooked the life out of my alfalfa and running to Almquist for a loan to take me through to next crop." He shook his head. "The trouble with farmers is that they don't farm like it was a business. Now you take Lotte. She's my daughter and she cleans and cooks and makes a fine home for us, but what if I didn't have her? I'd have to pay a housekeeper, wouldn't I?"

" 'Pears like."

"I do pay her," Keefer said. "Fifteen dollars a month and she gets to keep everything she makes off the chickens and the eggs. And that will run to nearly three hundred and fifty dollars a year." He nodded to include the hired men. "We've got an acre of vegetables, but we work it near sundown, when it's cooler. First off, we take what we need for the house, fill the root cellar out near the barn, fill the smoke house. The rest is sold in town and they split the profit. I get my share for the house by working. They take their share in money. What could be fairer than that?"

Temple smiled. "Tom, you're quite a guy, and now I know why: you know what the hell you're doin'. Be surprised how many men don't know what they're doin'." He leaned his elbows flat and traced a design with his fingers. "I like to know what I'm doin', Tom. That's why I came to see you. I've got three boys in jail charged with bank robbery and murder. Now I don't think they did it and I want to see them get a decent defense." He spread his hands. "No money for the lawyer."

"What makes you think they didn't do it?"

"A lot of reasons, and none of them sound like much. First, they were picked up in El Paso without a centavo. Now it ain't likely that they'd be stone broke. I can see 'em hidin' most of the money, but they'd keep out some, say thirty or forty dollars. Second, Almquist had a chance once to identify 'em and didn't. Now he's changed his mind. Third, Morgan had 'em in jail in town all the time he was out rammin' around making a big show of chasin' 'em." Keefer's attention was needle sharp; he invited Temple to go on with a slight nod. "Fourth, they claim Morgan let them out of jail and gave 'em two dollars apiece before putting them on the late freight to New Mexico. They could be lyin', but why invent a story as stupid as that? Tom, I want to get to the bottom of this and I need help."

"Suppose I call Rameras and Al Shannon and have 'em come over this evening?" Keefer said. "Won't hurt to talk to 'em, you know. They're reasonable men and they have their reasons for suspecting Morgan or Almquist."

CHAPTER
EIGHT

There was a remembered time in Jim Temple's youth when the arrival of cattle barons at a farmer's house meant an ultimatum, or shooting and burning; such a thing was out of the question now for they had learned to live together in friendship and peace, supporting one another and discovering that they made better partners than enemies.

Al Shannon and his oldest son arrived first; Keefer met them on the porch and ushered them inside. They shook hands with Jim Temple and Lotte served coffee, and they all sat down in Keefer's parlor.

Carlos Rameras arrived a few minutes later; he came in alone and the two men who rode with him went to the well curbing and waited there.

"It was nice of you to come here on such notice," Keefer said. "Jim, why don't I just let you do the talkin'?"

"All right, Tom." He snuffed out his cigaret. "My captain gave me this assignment because of a letter Tom wrote. He thought there was somethin' fishy about the robbery."

Carlos Rameras smiled; he was a giant of a man, dark skinned with thick gray hair and a mustache that was nearly white. "My friend, none of us liked it. It was done a bit too well."

"I've come to some conclusions myself," Temple said. "Now Ken Wallace says he and Almquist were seemingly alone in the bank; he says he looked at Almquist, or started to, then someone smacked him on the head. Almquist claims the boy's memory is shot. I don't think so because he's pretty clear on everything else you ask him about. Besides, why would he say there was no one? He could be confused and say there were four men, or six, or two, but he insists that there was no one, at least no one he saw. And I believe him."

Shannon nodded. "Ken's a good, reliable fella; I'd be inclined to believe him, blow on the head or no."

"So if we take Ken's word, we have to agree that Fred Almquist was lying. Now we're sure that he didn't hit Ken because Ken saw him just an instant before he was struck down. So there was a third man in the bank, and he wouldn't have been in the vault room without Almquist knowing it and approving it."

"I knew the sonof—" Keefer stopped and looked at his daughter. "Go ahead, Jim."

"So we come to the three men. Why did Almquist pick that number? As long as he was making it up, he could have said two or four. I figure it was no accident. I figure he saw the Adams boys loafing around and decided that here was three the world would never miss."

"How come no one else noticed 'em?" Shannon asked.

"Because they were on the bum and didn't want to attract attention to themselves," Temple said. "They came in on a late freight, riding the rods, and they laid low during the day in the freight yard and loading pens." He rolled another smoke while he talked. "All right, we've got Almquist using the Adams boys, but he couldn't just let them wander around; he had to control 'em and he couldn't do it himself."

"Miles Morgan," Keefer said, and Temple nodded.

"Maybe some easy money on Morgan's part, but he was in on it. The Adams boys went into Ben Perch's saloon, tried to cop some free lunch, got bawled out for it, and beat it out the back way. Morgan found them coming out of the alley and took them to the jail and locked 'em up in the cell block behind the storeroom. Then the robbery was discovered and Morgan made a big show of leading the posse."

Rameras' expression was grim. "Almquist robbed his own bank."

"He had some help," Temple said. "We don't know who, but he wasn't in this alone. Anyhow,

133

Morgan let the Adams boys out of jail a few days ago, then someone stuck a knife in him, figuring the Adams boys would be blamed for it. They were right. I brought them back from El Paso and they're in jail now. They're going to be tried for robbery and murder as sure as you're all sitting here." He paused to look around. "Which brings me to why I asked Tom to get us together. Those boys don't have a pot between 'em. The court will appoint a lawyer and since he won't be paid, he'll give them a pretty skimpy defense. They need money. A good lawyer. If they don't get it, they'll likely hang."

"How much?" Shannon asked.

Temple shrugged. "I was thinking about—fifteen hundred dollars?"

"That's a lot," Rameras said. "Quite a lot."

"Sure," Keefer said, "but if those boys are hung, the case is closed and Almquist has done it again. I'll put up five hundred. You, Al? Damn it, it's an investment in the community, the way I look at it. Can't you see that?"

For a moment Shannon thought about it. "All right, I'm in. Carlos?"

"I would hate to be left out."

Jim Temple was called to testify before the grand jury when it convened on Monday; he stayed a little better than an hour and was questioned thoroughly about the various phases of his investigation. Since the testimony was secret, he had no idea what went on, although he knew that Almquist testified, and Hub Riley, and Ken Wallace.

There were others, and he knew nothing would be settled that night so he went to bed early. The next day Tom Keefer and Lotte came to town.

Keefer had fifteen hundred dollars and wanted to telegraph an attorney in San Angelo who was making quite a reputation for himself. He and Jim Temple worded a letter, explaining the situation, and enclosing seven hundred and fifty dollars for a retainer, and Lotte took the sealed envelope to the post office while Keefer and Temple sat on the hotel porch and talked.

The jury was dismissed at a quarter to four and in ten minutes everyone in town had the news: the Adams brothers had been indicted for murder and bank robbery and were being held for trial.

The verdict was no surprise to Temple, but it made Tom Keefer angry. He swore a little and promised some trouble for Fred Almquist the next time he saw him and Temple didn't think much about it because Keefer was always carrying on this way about something, a big wind but never carrying much dust.

Then Fred Almquist came into view and as soon as he saw him, Keefer lunged off the porch and blocked the man's progress along the sidewalk.

"I want to say something to you," Keefer said flatly and gave him a push.

"Now you stop that!" Almquist said.

Jim Temple left his chair and started toward them, but Keefer wasn't waiting; he fisted some of Almquist's coat and hit him in the mouth, the force of the blow driving him back, tearing the coat because Keefer wouldn't let go.

Hub Riley boomed into view; Temple never did find out where from. Riley jerked Keefer back, then struck him alongside the head with a shot-loaded sap, stunning him, dropping him in the street. Then he snapped on a pair of handcuffs and hauled him to his feet, cuffing him twice in the face with an open hand.

"That's enough of that!" Temple snapped and Riley looked at him.

Fred Almquist was dabbing at the blood on his split lip. "I want that man arrested!" he yelled, attracting a crowd.

"He's already arrested," Temple said. "Go on home now." He took Hub Riley by the arm, and not gently. "You hit him again, sheriff, and I'll roll that tin badge up like a cigaret and stick it where you sit."

"He's going to jail," Riley said flatly.

"I didn't say he wasn't, but walk him there. Don't kick him."

Riley's dark eyes grew angry, but he said nothing more, just turned Tom Keefer and marched him off toward the jail at the point of his pistol. Temple turned slowly and looked at the gathered crowd and they suddenly remembered unfinished chores elsewhere. As he turned to go back to the porch he saw Lotte hurry along and he went to meet her.

There just wasn't any sense in being tactful; he told her straight out that Tom had acted like a damned fool and now he was in jail because of it.

"Him and his temper," she said. "Won't he ever learn?"

Jim Temple puckered his eyebrows. "Funny thing, but that storm blew up mighty fast. One minute he was sittin' there and the next—" He let it trail off.

"What's the matter?"

"After supper I'll go see him at the jail. Tom's too smart a man to pull a dumb stunt. I've watched him goad Morgan too many times, seen him come right up to that line and never step over it. It used to make Morgan furious." He took her arm and led her to the shade. "How about my buying your supper?"

"Can I have ice cream on my pie?" She had that wrinkle-nosed smile, and she watched him while he considered it very gravely.

"Why not?" he said. "We ought to whoop it up a little."

There was a good sized lump on the side of Tom Keefer's head and a dull ache began to expand the bones of his skull. He was in a cell next to the

Adams brothers and he sat up on the bunk, groaning a little at what the effort had cost him.

The Adams brothers watched him, but said nothing. Keefer looked at them and asked, "Which one of you is Woody?"

The oldest tapped himself on the chest.

"Can't you talk?" Keefer asked.

"Nothin' to say," Woody admitted.

"You fellas are in some real trouble," Keefer said cautiously.

"Mister, you ain't exactly a visitor yourself," Woody said.

Keefer smiled. "Friend, I'll be out in the morning, but you won't. Tell you what. I've got some friends who can get you out of this, but they'd want a cut of the bank money."

Woodrow Adams laughed. "Mister, if a train ride to Dallas cost five cents, we wouldn't have enough between the three of us to get out of town. There never was any money. Period."

"Ain't you charged with bank robbery?"

"In this crazy town you can be charged with anything, but that don't make it so." He settled back on his bunk. "Leave us alone, mister. We've got enough troubles to last us awhile."

"I hear you stabbed the sheriff," Keefer said.

"Yeah? And I hear the moon's made of green cheese."

"The talk I heard is that you stabbed him when he came in and bent down over your cot," Keefer said. "Then he staggered out to the front and fell."

"That's what the sheriff keeps tellin' us," Woody said, "but it don't make much difference how many times he says it; it just never happened. None of us stabbed anybody. We don't even own a knife between us except a small pen knife that Otis carried."

"And the new sheriff took that away from me," Otis said. "He's sure a mean cuss, always beltin' someone for somethin'. What did you do, mister? Spit on the sidewalk?"

"Fight."

"You're too old for that," Woody said. "Ought to have better sense. How do you expect us young people to behave if you old fellas set such a terrible example?"

"I wanted to get in here and talk to you," Keefer admitted. "And I figured it was the best way. Now if I'd walked in and talked through the bars you wouldn't have trusted me."

"What makes you think we will now?"

"Because I went to a lot of trouble. And Jim Temple will be in to cuss me out. We're tryin' to help you boys. Wish you'd believe it."

"We'd sure like to," Otis admitted. "But we're just nobody."

"There's some good men in this town who'll do their best by you," Keefer said. He stopped talking when the door to the cell block opened and Jim Temple stepped in. Hub Riley was with him and Temple turned and looked at the sheriff.

"I know my way, Riley."

"Well, I've got a rule—"

"Change it," Temple advised.

"You're going to push me one day and—" He made a cutting motion with his hand and turned and went back to his office.

Temple walked the length of the barred corridor and looked in on Tom Keefer. "If I didn't know you better I'd say you pulled a dumb stunt." His glance touched the Adams brothers. "Tom been talkin' some?"

"Yeah, some," Woody admitted. "Is he on the up and up, sergeant?"

"Oh, yes. He's feisty and hard to get along with, but if he says something, it's so. We're gettin' you a lawyer from San Angelo. A good man who'll work hard for you."

"How come?" Otis wanted to know.

Temple looked at them. "Look now, pride can take you right up a gallows steps."

"I guess," Woody said, "but when you're down on your luck like we are, pride's all you've got left."

"Then make sure it isn't false pride," Temple advised. "I've arranged bail for you, Champ. And I might as well tell you I did it to please Lotte; she didn't like the idea of you spending the night in here."

"Why, I think that's the sweetest thing," Keefer said.

"I'll go post your bail," Temple told him and went into Hub Riley's office. The man was sitting with the swivel chair tilted back, his feet on the desk; he was paring his fingernails with a large Mexican spring knife and he put it away when Jim Temple stepped in.

"The justice of the peace said twenty dollars." He dropped the bill on Riley's desk. "A receipt and then let Keefer out."

"How do I know—"

"Because I just told you." He waited and then Riley wrote out the receipt and Temple pocketed it. Riley got his keys and went back and brought Keefer out, giving him one final shove.

The old man turned his head and said, "You have a hard time keepin' your hands off people, don't you, Riley? A big temper, ain't you? All wound up inside and ready to let go any time, ain't you?"

"You'd better learn to shut your big mouth," Riley advised. He waved his hand. "Get out of here."

"Don't need a second invite for that," Keefer murmured and stepped out, but Temple remained behind; he toed the door closed and sat down on the edge of the desk.

"That get out was for you too," Riley said.

"I thought you'd like to throw me out. No? Then we'll talk. I never did get it clear just where you were when the sheriff was killed."

"Off duty. I forget where I was. Around town some place."

"That doesn't sound too definite."

"It's all you'll get," Riley warned. "I've told you a couple of times not to push me. I won't take it."

"You're lettin' your temper show again. You know, Keefer kind of hit on it, didn't he? You're always churnin' inside, smoke comin' out your nose, always holdin' back, ready to let go. Now just what would happen if you did let go, Riley? Would you kill somebody?"

"You're talking crazy."

"Sure now, real crazy. I knew Morgan, better than you ever did. He was a hard man to work for. He liked to boss things, give orders. Everything he did, he did big, like it was a grandstand move and he could hear the crowd cheering. And he was afraid of all men, Riley. That's why he had to boss them, always tellin' them off to do dirty little jobs; it made him feel a little bigger." He smiled and let his eyes pull into narrow, meaty slits; he watched Riley with an unwavering brightness. "I'll bet that used to boil you, huh? Sending you on errands. I'll bet you it was one of those hot muggy nights when it happened. Morgan had the Adams boys locked up; you knew about them but you were smart enough to keep your mouth shut about it. Anyway, Morgan had let the boys go; it was late and they were catching the New Mexico freight out of town. While Morgan was gone, you came back here." He never took his eyes off Riley's set face. "You and Morgan got into a jangle. Probably it started over nothing, something Morgan said; he was always pickin' on a man's weakness. You were back in the corridor and suddenly that tightness inside you let go and you let him have it with your knife. Morgan clapped his hands to his belly and staggered back." Temple suddenly began to smile. "Yeah, Riley, you got up off the floor. You'd had a little scuffle and you stabbed him when you were down. Morgan had a way of pushing people around that you in particular wouldn't like; he'd bump a man with his belly. It was kind of a trademark with him, bouncing people off his belly like rubber balls. That must have made you blow up, huh, Riley? What were you doin'? Standin' in his way? He knocked you down and you stabbed him. Then he staggered out here to the office and fell."

He stopped talking and for a full mute minute, Hub Riley sat there, his hands splayed out on the desk top.

Temple let it soak in, then said, "You know how I know, Riley? Because the boys didn't do it. Morgan was alive when they left here. There wasn't anyone else who could have done it." He got up slowly and looked down at Riley. "You know I'm right, and I know I can't prove it, but that's not going to stop me. You know that too. Look at my eyes, Riley. What do you see there?

You sit here on your cracker ass and think about running for election, but I'll tell you the real truth; you're not going to live until election."

"You can't bluff me, Temple."

"Why, now, I never intended to do that, Riley. Tell you what. If the Adams boys hang for this killing, you can count the days you have left to live on both hands. Because I'll get you, Riley. I'll drive you, run at you, until you make a break. When I get through you'll walk backward to see who's back there and wish all the time you could see what's ahead. There won't be a leaf that'll rustle and not make you pee your pants. Dark alleys will be something you won't have guts enough to walk by. Then you're going to break inside and come for me and I'll be waitin' and then you won't have to worry about anything any more."

Temple talked softly, never letting his eyes leave Riley's face, and he watched the sheen of sweat on the man's forehead and upper lip. Then he slapped his hand down suddenly on the desk and Riley jumped and hated himself for displaying this weakness.

"So you watch yourself, huh, Riley?"

He turned and stepped outside and found Keefer waiting at the base of the steps. "You two had a lot to talk about," Keefer said.

"I was just explaining to Hub how he killed Morgan." He had taken a step on, then he stopped and looked back; Keefer was standing with his mouth open. "Well, he did do it, Tom. Who else could have done it?"

"Hell, a dozen men in this town—"

"A dozen like Riley?" He shook his head and they walked on together. "For a time there I just couldn't figure it out, why there wasn't any blood back there in the cell blocks. A man will drop some blood almost the moment he's wounded. You've seen it on the farm, Tom; a man hurts himself and stands there a minute, tryin' to figure out what happened, and he'll bleed a little. Hell, the heart's in there pumpin' away, squirtin' it out. No, there just wasn't any blood at all except halfway down the corridor, then leadin' into the office, gettin' worse as Morgan staggered to the front of the building." He looked at Tom Keefer. "It was a bull's-eye guess. Riley turned the color of curd. He knows I'm out to put salt on his tail, and it'll make him jumpy."

"Jumpy enough to waylay you," Keefer said as they turned into the hotel. Lotte was at a table in the dining room and they sat down and gave their order to the waiter.

"Hello, jailbird," she said. "How's your head?"

"Beating steadily."

"You're just too old to fight, papa."

Keefer bristled and mulched his false teeth against his gums. "Damn it, I wish people would stop tellin' me that." He pulled down the volume of his voice and looked around sheepishly. "Why is it I'm destined to always make a fool of myself?" He looked at Temple and found him smiling. "That seem funny to you?"

"Yeah," Temple admitted. "You're an old bull who still paws up an acre of pasture and never gets over the fence to the cow."

"Now that's a hell of a thing to say," Keefer opined. "I'm going down to the drug store and get me some headache tablets." He got up. "While I'm at it, I may even take a liver purge."

"See if they've got any smart pills," Temple suggested.

"Why? Are you out?" He laughed at his own joke and left, walking as though he were marching in a parade.

The waiter came with their roast beef and looked questioningly at Keefer's empty chair. Temple said, "Leave it, he'll be back."

"I'll keep it warm in the oven." The waiter took it back and they spent a moment passing salt and pepper and sugar and butter back and forth, then Lotte put her hand on her mouth and laughed.

"I take it there's a joke in this some place?"

"Look over there." He followed her glance and watched another couple passing the salt and sugar and cream and all the time trying to cut their steak, take that first bite; it was a demonstration in frustration and cultivated patience.

"I'll bet we looked like that," she said.

"Oh, I don't know," Temple said. "I think I'm better lookin' than he is. My reach is longer too." He kept the smile off his face but not out of his eyes. "Tell you what, we'll count to ten, then start eating on signal."

"That sounds good. Want me to count?"

"Ladies first."

She began and some other diners turned and looked at her but she was very serious about it and Jim Temple watched her and wondered just why the devil he hadn't noticed all these wonderful things about her before. Then he decided that he had noticed, but suddenly they were in sharp focus and much better that way.

". . . Ten," she said and deftly sliced the roast beef, her knife squeaking across the plate.

"That isn't allowed," he said. "Do it again and I'll have to ask you to leave the table. I'm sensitive."

"Oh, I know and I'm dreadfully sorry. Would it be all right if I slapped myself?" She tried to keep her face straight, but couldn't and when she laughed a plump woman one table over turned her head slowly and stared. Lotte said, "Your underskirt is showing."

There was a gasp, a look of horror and the woman bent forward, bosom crushed against the edge of the table and complained in a soft, droning voice to her husband.

Tom Keefer came back and sat down. "Heard a rumor while I was at the drugstore."

"There are diamonds in our creek," Lotte suggested.

Keefer frowned. "Ain't you ever serious?" He glanced at Jim Temple. "Harry Randall ain't goin' to prosecute. They're bringin' in a lawyer, a senator from Webb County. Lon Barrett." He rolled his eyes. "Plug your ears, gran'ma; they're wheelin' in the big artillery."

CHAPTER
NINE

Stanley Franklin was a rather tall man, very slender, with thin, delicate fingers and he had the habit of playing constantly with his watch fob. He sat in the hotel room Jim Temple had taken when he first came to town and he looked at Temple, then at Tom Keefer.

"You didn't tell me Lon Barrett was prosecuting the case."

"Does it make a difference?" Keefer asked.

"It certainly has political overtones," Franklin admitted.

"Are you afraid of it?" Temple asked frankly.

The attorney shrugged; he was in his late thirties, a fine dresser, and a man with his eye on distant stars. "My concern is the selecting of an impartial jury. How do the people here feel?"

"They haven't marched on the jail, if that's what you mean," Temple said. "They feel that since an arrest has been made and charges filed, they'll leave it to the court to convict the guilty and recover their money. I think you can get a good jury."

Franklin nodded and made a business of lighting

a cigar. Then he glanced at them, a quick, passing flick of his pale eyes. "You are convinced that the Adams brothers are innocent?" They both nodded. "But no proof."

"No, but neither can Barrett prove they're guilty."

"From your letter, I'd say there was a good deal of circumstantial evidence," Franklin said.

"You're being paid damned well to win the case, in spite of it," Keefer pointed out.

Franklin nodded in agreement. "And Lon Barrett is going to make a big effort to win it. Already the newspapers are devoting a lot of space to it; I even read about it in the San Antone paper. Either way, the case will have political significance. Carefully played, these three boys could very well become as famous as the James brothers. The charge is bank robbery and murder, gentlemen, certainly major crimes that could carry the death penalty. If Lon Barrett wins this case, every man of voting age in the state will know his name and his picture will be in half the papers."

"That works both ways, Mr. Franklin," Temple pointed out.

The man's eyebrows went up briefly. "Oh, I know. If I win it, I can go back to my own county and run for state legislature and win. Some very successful careers have been based on less. You see, to run for public office people have to know you. That means you have to draw attention to yourself through civic work or professional reputation, which is the likely route for me."

Tom Keefer looked a bit disgusted. "Ain't there one of you fellas who ain't after somethin'?"

"Why shouldn't we be?" Franklin asked. "You're after something. You want the boys cleared of the charges."

"The difference is, it's for someone beside myself."

"Is it really?" Franklin laughed. "Gentlemen, pardon my cynicism, but I just don't believe people are good all the time." His glance touched Jim Temple. "You gentlemen in the Texas Rangers enjoy a pretty broad reputation, but someday, someone is going to be bribed, or betray you and then you'll find there's nothing to hold you up or keep you going and you'll be what you really are, underpaid, understaffed cops." He observed Temple's reaction and laughed. "Gentlemen, understand me. I don't give a good damn if the Adams brothers are guilty or innocent. I took the case because the fee was good and because winning it is important to me. And that is reason enough for a man to do anything."

Keefer shook his head. "I thought—"

"Yes," Franklin interrupted, "I know what you thought. You thought you were buying idealism. I must disappoint you. You'll find that only in very young lawyers just admitted to the bar, but they soon learn that the rent has to be paid and that

151

idealism pays poorly. Believe me, you don't want that kind of a man." He got up and knocked a long ash off his cigar. "No, gentlemen, I will not disappoint you. I fight for my clients, right or wrong, and I fight fair or foul. Now, I believe I'll go and talk to my clients. I trust they're all simple, honest men?"

"Yes," Temple said, "and you won't understand them."

"I know that," Stanley Franklin said, "but I can still give them a good defense."

After he left, Tom Keefer let his aggravation show. "Now ain't he somethin'? Huh?" He shook his head. "If I'd known about him personally I'd—"

"I think he'll do the job," Temple said, closing Keefer out. "He'll fight dirty if he has to. And ain't that what Almquist and Riley are doin'? Come on, let's get some supper and head out to your place; I want to get out of town for awhile."

Keefer's room was down the hall and they picked Lotte up there and walked down the broad stair to the dining room. The waiter smiled and gave them the same table they'd had the night before and he took their order. Temple noticed that a larger than usual crowd was in the dining room and he supposed that these people were drawn here by the trial, reporters and magazine writers, all after a story with a handle that would catch up reader interest and sell advertising.

He was letting his glance circulate around the room when he saw Martha Ivers stop just inside the archway and for a moment he couldn't believe it. She wore a dark dress, tight at the waist, with just enough bare shoulder to make men look and women not become envious.

She saw him and smiled and came over, passing gracefully between the crowded tables; Temple stood up and handed her into a chair. "Martha, this is my friend, Tom Keefer, and his daughter, Lotte. Martha Ivers." He sat down. "What the devil are you doing here? Did you come up with the senator?"

"Yes, we arrived on the afternoon train."

"Is it, missus or—"

"Still miss," she said and looked at Lotte. "My, how pretty you are. I just knew Jim had a girl here." Her glance touched Temple. "I should be mad at you, Jim. If you hadn't arrested those men, I think I might have led Lon to the altar a month ahead of schedule. Until he says, 'I do,' he can always change his mind. And women do worry about that, you know. Especially this one."

"There's a man on every corner," Keefer said.

"Yes, but not one like Lon Barrett. They tell me that once he fell off his wallet and broke his arm. And it's just as easy for a woman to love a man with money than one—"

"Oh, cut it out, Martha," Temple said. "You're not like that."

"Just what is she like, Jim?" Lotte asked in a tone that chilled the water glasses.

Martha Ivers rolled her eyes. "Men are so stupid. Including you, Jim."

"Well, just what did I do?" He was immediately indignant.

She ignored him and spoke to Lotte. "I couldn't help notice your expression when Jim introduced us. Well, I'm as honest as you are and I wanted to say, as cleverly as I could, that I didn't have any hold on this paragon of law and order. But that's not saying that I hadn't thought about it. Maybe some other time, some other place—" She shrugged her shoulders. "It doesn't surprise me that we should both like men with rough edges."

"I understand," Lotte said, "and I'm sorry. I really am."

"No need to be," Martha Ivers said. "I'm going to marry Lon Barrett and I'm still a little jealous of you now."

Temple's flustered attention was on Martha and Lotte and he didn't see Hobo Teal approach the table until he spoke. He nodded to the ladies and said, "Jim, hate to bother you, but I got a message from Nora Shannon. She wants to see you, right away, if you can come."

"Well, I guess I can, if it's important. Is she in town?"

Teal shook his head. "She wants you to ride out. You know that stand of timber to the north?

There's a line cabin there. She don't want her father to know about this, so I'm to take you there."

"What's this all about, Hobo?"

He shook his head again. "Danged if I know, but she says it's important." He rubbed his hands against the legs of his jeans. "You want me to get your horse and wait outside?"

"Yes, you do that," Temple said and watched him thread his way out.

Martha smiled. "Another woman, Jim? You know, I'm just beginning to get a real picture of you."

"Don't let your imagination run away with you," he said, taking the napkin out of his collar. "You go on home, Tom. I'll ride over as soon as I find out what this is all about."

"And you be sure to tell me what it's all about," Lotte suggested. "I'll really want to know." She looked at Martha Ivers. "Nora Shannon is not exactly what you'd call plain as a mud fence. In fact, she fills out her clothes very nicely."

"I'm glad I'm not suspicious natured," Temple said and got up from the table. Out of the corner of his eye he saw someone approaching and turned as Lon Barrett came up.

"Good to see you, Temple." He bent and kissed Martha on the cheek. "It seems that I often find you two together, my dear. Coincidence, of course."

"No, I came over and Jim introduced me. I didn't want to eat alone, Lon."

"I'm making a very bad joke," Barrett said and bowed when Martha introduced him to Lotte and her father. There was nothing to do but invite him to sit; he took Temple's chair, and Temple said good-bye and went outside. Hobo Teal was leading the horses down the street; they swung up and worked through the traffic and once they cleared the end of the street they lifted the horses into a trot and rode that way for nearly two miles.

Then they took a dirt road that led to Spindle. There was a quarter moon and some scudding clouds and low-backed hills framed this valley.

Hobo Teal stopped and pointed toward the northwest. "Cross that ridge and follow the trail for a couple of miles," he said. "The cabin's on the west fork of the creek. You'll see it at the edge of timber."

"I thought you was comin' along?"

Teal shook his head. "I said that for your woman's benefit."

"Hobo, you've been with Spindle a long time, haven't you?"

"Twenty years. Since 1890."

"Is there anything that goes on there that you don't know about?"

"Nope."

"I don't suppose you'd care to tell me anything?"

"Now, I just couldn't do that, Jim." He snapped

the brim of his hat and smiled. "I'll see you, huh?" He rode on before Temple could answer.

He watched him a moment, then turned his horse and cut up over the rise, a good fifteen-minute ride. Then he worked his way down the gentle slope and across another brush-covered valley toward a dark stand of timber yet a mile or so away. When he came to the creek he swung west, staying along the west fork until it branched. Then he stopped and studied the dark timber, finally making out the low outline of the cabin a few hundred yards beyond.

It was dark, but when he stepped down to tie his horse, he noticed another picketed around the corner. Then he caught movement in the dark doorway and Nora Shannon said, "Jim, is that you?"

"Yes." He walked to the door and she stepped back so that he could go inside. She fumbled for a lamp as soon as he closed the door and when she set the glass down on the base and the light steadied, he saw that hung blankets covered the windows.

He said, "Doesn't your father know you're away from the house?"

"He's in town. Staying over night."

Temple studied her, a tall, dark-haired woman in her middle twenties. She had a heart-shaped face with full lips and expressive brown eyes, and her figure was full enough to make most any man turn his head.

"This is kind of strange, Nora, meeting me out here."

"Shame makes you that way, Jim. It makes you seek out darkness and little used places. I just can't go it alone, Jim. I've got to have help." She sat down at the table and folded her hands.

"I expect you've figured out that I don't know what you're talkin' about," Temple said.

"You know how it was with Miles and me."

"No, I don't know. How could I know, Nora?"

She looked at him then, her expression pained. "But you must have guessed!"

He shook his head. "Those things I don't guess about."

"We used to meet here," she said in a small, listless voice. "When dad would go to town, I'd come here, and as soon as Miles saw him come in, he'd ride out. We spent nights here. I loved him with everything a woman has, Jim. It was two lives, really. One, the one we showed everyone, was polite and restrained; it was a very formal engagement. The other life?" She shrugged her shoulders. "It was so real that it lost all reality. It was just the two of us, alone on this earth, and we acted like it." She looked at him. "Doesn't that make you sick? I suppose the only difference between me and Thelma Scanlon is that it doesn't make her sick."

"She's never loved a man," Temple said. "That's a difference."

"Oh, I don't know, Jim. I suppose I always knew that Miles was lying to me, using me; a woman can really tell if she's honest enough. But I couldn't help myself. I still can't."

"You must have been takin' a big chance," Temple said. "I mean, what was goin' to keep a Spindle rider from droppin' in for a snooze and findin' you here with Miles?"

"Hobo gave them work that kept them away from here," Nora said. "He's always been my friend, Jim. He told me to talk to you." Her fingers entwined restlessly. "I've faced it, finally. I can admit now that Miles is dead; I've stopped denying it to myself." She got up and walked around the room. "I'll fix some coffee."

"You don't have to."

"It'll give me something to do," she said and lighted the fire in the sheet-iron stove. "Who killed Miles?" She filled the pot and looked at him. "Not those three men. I just don't believe that, Jim."

"No, they didn't do it. Nora, do you know anything about this?"

"Was it Hub Riley?" She set the pot over the fire and came back, standing in front of him, looking into his eyes. "Miles and Hub have known each other a long time, Jim. It goes quite a few years back. To other bank robberies. Hub gets twenty percent and Miles gets twenty percent and Almquist keeps the rest and any insurance that he

159

might be carrying." The heat was beginning to make the coffee pot rock and thump. "I was going to keep my mouth shut, Jim. Figure out any reason for it you like, but the truth is I was going to say nothing because I didn't have guts enough to stand up and say just how I knew all this. But Hub killed Miles and I'm not going to stand by and let him get away with it. Hub hit young Wallace on the head. I think the rest you can figure out for yourself."

"It's no good, just sayin' that, Nora. How do you know?" He waited for her to speak and when she didn't he said, "All right, let's forget it then. If you won't tell me, it's sure you won't stand up in court. It's just one of your dreams, Nora, to make you feel like a woman. And like a dream, it's not real."

He started to turn, to leave her, but she quickly took his arm. "No, don't go! All right. It was a year since Miles and I broke up. The most miserable year I ever spent. Then one night, I went to town with dad. He was expecting one of his prize mares to foal, and he had to go back right away. I stayed over. Then the idea came to me, so strong I couldn't put it out of my mind, and I went to the hotel, using the back stairs and got into Miles' room. All I could think about was how it would be when we were together again, and then I heard him outside; he had someone with him, a man. Jim, I was panic stricken, so I hurried and hid in the closet. Miles talked to this man—I later learned that it was Hub Riley—and they were talking about the robbery, and just how it was going to be pulled off. What they were waiting for was some drifter to come through to pin it on. I heard it all, Jim, then they went out. I was shaking so bad I couldn't leave right away, so I waited about twenty minutes. Then Miles came back before I could leave. He had Thelma Scanlon with him." She put her hands to her face and stood there and Temple went over and rescued the coffee pot from the heat. He got two tin cups from the cupboard and a can of condensed milk, making two punch holes with an icepick stuck in the wall. He brought the coffee to the table and put a cup in front of her.

"You want to go on or leave it up to my imagination?"

"I hid in that closet for three hours, Jim." She shuddered and raised her coffee cup. "Then I saw myself, knew what it had really been like here. When I could leave, I did. I came home and I've stayed there."

Temple thought about it, then said, "Nora, could you take the stand in court and repeat this?"

"I'd like to think that I could," she said. "God, how I'd like to think that."

"If you did, there wouldn't be much left for you here," Temple said.

"Yes, I know. That's why I had to talk to you,

Jim. I trust you. I believe you'd tell me which was the right thing."

"You already know that."

"Yes, but can I?"

"Miles is dead, and Hub Riley would deny it. It could be that you'd be throwin' everything away for nothin'." He wiped a hand over his cheek and fingered his mustache. "Then too, if Riley knew that you overheard the conversation, he might try to kill you."

"I'm not afraid of dying. I think that it may be the best thing."

"Now that's kind of feeling sorry for yourself," Temple said bluntly. "Nora, you're a grown woman. You knew what you were doin' when you came here with Miles. To tell you the truth, I don't like it. You could have said somethin' before and cleared those three men, but you kept your mouth shut. Now you'll talk, not because you want to see justice done, but because you want to avenge a man who wasn't good enough for any woman. I've always been honest with you, and I'll give it to you straight now: you do what you want to do. But you remember that a lawyer like Lon Barrett's going to take you apart on the stand. When he finishes with you, about the only place you could go is one of the Mexican cribs along the border for ten cents a throw. The newspapers will have a holiday with you. And you'll give your father and two brothers something they'll never live down."

He drank most of his coffee then put the cup aside and got up. "Nora, I don't feel a damned bit sorry for you. All this you stepped into with your eyes open, selfishly, to get out of it as much as you could. Then you want to figure too that I'm not sure I believe you. You've lied to your dad and to Hobo Teal, who never once helped you because it was his job. You've lied to yourself all along. And I wouldn't be surprised but what you've lied to Morgan."

"You certainly don't think much of me, do you, Jim?"

"How much do you think of yourself?"

"I hate myself now," she said.

"Did you ever do anything, just once, that wasn't for yourself?"

She watched him steadily. "I—can't remember, Jim. That's terrible, isn't it?"

"Yeah, it sure is." He turned to the door, opened it and went outside and mounted his horse. He took the same route back and when he came to the fork in the creek he found a horseman waiting there.

Then the man struck a match to light his smoke and Temple could make his recognition. He said, "I thought you went on, Hobo?"

"Changed my mind."

"If you want to be with her, don't wait here."

"She don't want me," Teal said. "This is close enough." He pulled on his cigarette and the end glowed brightly. "I'll just stay close enough to see that no harm comes to her."

This made Temple angry. "Why, you damned fool! What more could come to her? You're doin' her no favor, pickin' up her marbles and blowin' her nose."

"I do what I think's right."

"It's wrong!"

"My decision," Teal said stubbornly.

"Then if you're goin' to make decisions, use your brains a little. God damn it, you had no business fixin' it so she could have her parties in the cabin. Is that all she is to you, some cheap whore?"

"Don't talk to me that way," Hobo Teal warned. "Don't you ever talk about her that way or I'll kill you!"

Temple let disgust fill his voice. "Hobo, don't give me that brave crap. I've seen pimps who were better than you. What the hell were you thinkin' about when she was out here bouncin' her ass for Miles?"

Teal leaped off his horse at Temple, who batted him aside with a clenched fist, knocking him asprawl in the grass; he jumped down as Teal scrambled to his feet and took a bouncing fist off his forehead in order to smash Teal alongside the jaw, dropping him again.

Before Teal could get up, Temple had both knees on his chest, pinching off his wind, hurting him a little. He fisted some of Teal's hair and banged his head into the earth a few times.

"Now you listen to me, Hobo. Listen or by God I'll put some lumps on you. Don't hold her up any more. Make her stand and she may be a woman yet, at least one that's worth havin'. All the hurt that's come to her she's done herself, to herself. She's got to quit that or she's nothin'. You understand that?"

"Let me up," Teal said.

"Behave yourself?" He waited and Teal nodded; Temple got off him and picked up his hat, then handed Teal his. "You cooled off enough to think straight?"

"I guess," Hobo Teal said. "All the years I've known her, Jim, I've tried to smooth out the bumps for her."

"You took her responsibility away from her," Temple said flatly. "You made her think that whatever she did, you'd make it right if it didn't come out that way."

"I've wanted to kill Morgan myself," Teal said. "He was no good for her."

"That's not the truth. You tell me really what's the truth now."

Teal hesitated. "I guess she wasn't good for herself, Jim." He nodded his head and touched the bruised spot on his jaw. "I want to go to her now, but I guess I can't, huh? You want to ride a way with me?"

"Sure," Temple said and remounted.

They turned back together and when Teal looked around, Temple said, "You've got to learn not to do that any more, Hobo. If she makes it, she'll see you. Really see you. If she's worth anything it'll work out fine."

"Like to believe it," Teal said.

"You might as well," Temple told him. "What else is there?"

CHAPTER
TEN

Lon Barrett rented a suite of rooms at the hotel; he liked to live splendidly and he introduced Martha Ivers around as his fiancée and social secretary because he planned to entertain frequently during his stay. He had a bar brought up to his suite and a man put on duty to serve his guests, and almost constantly there was someone coming and going, someone who had something to talk over with the senator, or just wanted to shake hands.

That evening, around ten o'clock, the hotel employee was dismissed and Martha Ivers acted as hostess because Barrett was still entertaining. Fred Almquist was there, and Stanley Franklin; they had drinks and comfortable chairs, and then Lyle Pollack knocked and was let in. He gave Martha his hat and said, "I'm terribly sorry I'm late. My wife—"

"No explanation necessary," Barrett said, smiling. "Martha, fix Mr. Pollack a drink."

"Thank you, but I shouldn't. My wife—" He shrugged and smiled. "Well, perhaps just a small one." He watched Martha Ivers while she dropped ice in a glass, then with an effort pulled his attention back to Senator Barrett.

"It certainly was nice of you gentlemen to accept my invitation," Barrett said. He raised his glass. "To the trial, gentlemen. May it be speedy and just."

They drank to that and Barrett put his glass down and clasped his hands behind him. "I've had cases I've liked better." He looked at Stanley Franklin. "You really don't have much of a defense."

"No, but neither have you a sound basis to prosecute," Franklin said. "It's very thin, senator. If you're not careful, the judge may throw it out."

"You intend to ask for a dismissal, of course."

Franklin nodded. "Of course. Wouldn't you?"

Barrett laughed softly. "Yes, I certainly would. However, I think there's more to consider here than legal procedure. The case has attracted a good deal of public interest all over the state. I think it's much too important to handle carelessly." He handed his glass to Martha. "Would you refresh this, my dear? Thank you. First off, gentlemen, we've lost the bank. Mr. Almquist tells me that there is some insurance and when he collects it he plans to open, establish credit to many of the citizens who are hard pressed for cash. This is, and I want you to keep it in mind, in the best interests of the public. And that's who we're dedicated to serving, the public."

"I wouldn't argue with you there," Franklin

said. "When is the insurance company going to pay off?"

"They'll withhold it until the outcome of the trial," Almquist said. "If it's prolonged—" He shrugged and spread his hands. "Before, they've withheld payment for nearly a year. I think that there are merchants in town who could not survive that long."

"Well, it's tough," Stanley Franklin admitted, "but I must think of my clients first. Senator, you understand that I'm sure."

"Of course, and in a way I'm thinking of them first," Barrett said. "Gentlemen, we have a positive identification of the three men. That's going to be hard to argue against, counselor."

"I believe Mr. Almquist is honestly mistaken."

Barrett spread his hands and smiled. "But that's a matter for the courts to adjudicate. It's going to be a fight, Mr. Franklin." He sipped his drink. "It's my hope that we can be realistic about this, citizen. I'm sure you'll agree that it's better all around if we do."

"What is your definition of realistic, senator?"

"A change of plea."

Franklin laughed. "Not on your life."

"Suppose I said that I intended to introduce another eyewitness who could make a positive identification in support of Mr. Almquist's testimony." Barrett studied him carefully. "I'd blow your case right out the window, citizen."

"You don't have one," Franklin said. "Young Wallace—" He stopped talking and looked at the empty glass he held in his hand.

"That's right," Barrett said. "Ken Wallace's memory came back. Clear as a bell, citizen. Kind of rocks you, doesn't it? Now I could have waited and sprung that on you in court, but I hate to see a good man wasted like that." He sat down and folded his hands and looked steadily at Stanley Franklin. "Citizen, I think it's best for everyone if we terminate this as quickly as possible. Why drag it out when you can't get an acquittal anyway? You're a bright man, Franklin, and people are taking notice of you. If you played your cards right, you'd be a superior judge in no time."

"Are you offering me something, senator?"

"I'm pointing out some likely possibilities," Barrett said. "You could become a justice of the state supreme court, citizen, but you won't make it being stubborn." He leaned back and ticked off the points on his fingers. "First, I believe a jury trial would be foolish; the whole thing should be left in Judge Hanlon's hands. Secondly, I think the charge of murder should be dismissed, and at the same time I believe the court would accept a plea of guilty to robbery. Hanlon is a just, humane man. Under the circumstances, I think he'd hand down a minimum sentence: five years."

"That's well thought out, senator."

"Oh, not really. If I take it to court and win it,

you can bet your Blackstone that I'll push for twenty years. This is a chance to give your clients the best possible break, Franklin. You know it is too."

Franklin took out a package of cigarets and lit one. "Senator, I don't suppose you'd let a man think about this?"

"No, because there's nothing to think about." He smiled. "What did you want to do? Check with Wallace?" He shook his head. "You can give me your answer now, citizen."

Stanley Franklin looked around the room; they were very quiet. Martha Ivers stood back near the bar, her expression showing him nothing. He took a final drag on his cigaret and snuffed it out. Then he sighed and said, "All right, senator." He got up and Martha gave him his hat and Franklin went to the door, put his hand on the knob, then turned his head and looked long at Lon Barrett. "When do you think I ought to order my robes, senator?"

"It won't be long, citizen."

Franklin went out, closing the door very quietly, and for a moment no one said anything, then Fred Almquist tipped his head back and laughed. It built a quick anger in Lon Barrett's eyes and he snapped, "Shut your damned mouth!"

Almquist stared at him. "Don't talk to me like that."

"And don't sit there and laugh because you've

seen a man sell himself." He waved his hand. "All right, get out. The party is over."

Pollack, never at ease in the first place, went out first. Fred Almquist lingered a moment, his glance going to Martha Ivers; he had something he wanted to say but he didn't want her to hear it and because she was there he held it back; he nodded and left.

Barrett went over and poured himself another drink. "I hated to do that to Franklin."

"Did you, Lon?"

"Yes, I did. I've made the same kind of compromises and I know how he feels." He put his hand on her cheek and patted it. "Don't think badly of me, Martha. Business is not always nice." He let his hand fall away. "Better go to your room now."

"Goodnight, Lon."

She did not kiss him; she left and walked down the hall to the stairs and slowly went up; her room was on the second floor, halfway down and she fitted her key and went in, not bothering to turn on the lights. She was tired but she knew that she could not sleep, and kept remembering the look on Fred Almquist's face as Barrett had talked; the man seemed to be holding his breath and she wondered why.

Without knowing for sure, she knew that Lon Barrett had run a bluff when he said that Ken Wallace could support Almquist's identification.

It was a lie, convincingly told, and it made her wonder how much he really lied; any man that could do it so well would not stick to the truth because truth was always so confining, and a man like Lon Barrett just didn't like to be confined.

She stretched out on the bed, still fully clothed and listened to the sounds that filtered up through the street and thought about herself. Her parents were dead and her only relative was an aunt in Taos, New Mexico; she was alone and she didn't mind that, yet there is an element of terror in it for a woman; they could not live without men; they needed a man's name and his reputation and a home.

Her father had been a hard-working man, a saving man, and when he died he left a few thousand dollars, a small house, and few prospects for the future. Martha Ivers had a choice and she made it. She sold the house, took the savings and moved to San Francisco. By careful buying, careful management of her social life, she met Lon Barrett, a man she could admire tremendously, and she became engaged to him.

It was the only thing a woman could do, an honorable thing, for she had liked him and knew that she could make him happy without making herself miserable; this was a compromise most women ambitious enough to marry well could not make.

Now it was all wrong. The teachings of an

honest bricklayer came up like a wet towel in the face, jolting her, taking her right back to that small frame house in Sacramento, California, and she felt ill.

At eleven thirty she left her room very quietly and walked down the hall toward the back; she knew that Jim Temple's room was there and she knocked insistently but there was no answer. For a moment she could not decide what to do. She wondered if he were in town, but then she decided that he was not. He was probably at Tom Keefer's farm and she knew only the general direction because he had described it while they were having dinner.

Her thought was to go back to her room, but she knew she couldn't do that; she'd made up her mind about something now and she knew it was right and nothing would change it.

Using the back stairs, she let herself into the alley, walked the length of it, then stopped and looked at some saddle horses tied along the side street. She had never ridden except when she had been very small and then someone had always held her on to keep her from falling, but there was no time to think of that now.

Untying the horse, she tried to put her foot in the stirrup, but her dress hooked her at the knee and she had to hoist her skirt high to get aboard. Then she almost fell off on the other side, and clung to the mane.

The horse, unaccustomed to a woman rider, snorted and begun to fuss and she prayed that he wouldn't pitch. The stirrups were too long; she couldn't reach them, but she kicked the horse with her heels and he started down the street and forgot about bucking her off.

A mile out of town she knew she couldn't go on. The continual bouncing on the hard saddle was too much for her; she knew she had hurt herself a way back and finally she sawed the reins and the horse stopped and she half fell, half slid off and lay in the grass. The horse immediately turned and went back to town.

She got up and stood there a moment, hurting and confused, then she took a bearing and started walking. She followed the dusty road for almost a mile, then her feet began to hurt and she stopped and took off her shoes and stockings, carrying them in her hand as she limped along. She was very sore from the bouncing in the saddle and when she came to a creek she stopped and sat down in the shallows near the shore, letting the cold water revive her.

In the silence she heard a bell sheep in the distance and she got up and went on, and finally she saw Keefer's place on the rise. When she came to the fence she didn't bother with searching out the gate; she climbed it and walked across a pasture. There were sheep in it and she disturbed them and they ran. This sound alerted a dog and he ran out, barking and setting up a clamor.

Lights came on and then she climbed the fence to the yard and Tom Keefer and his two hired hands met her; Jim Temple came from the house too and he had a lantern in his hand, holding it high so that a puddle of yellow light fell around him.

Tom Keefer picked her up and carried her inside with surprising ease, bellowing for Lotte. Temple went ahead and opened the kitchen door and Lotte came out in a thin cotton nightgown.

"Well for heaven's sake. Take her in my room, Pa." She stood back and Keefer went in and laid Martha Ivers on the bed. "Put on some coffee, Pa." She gave him a gentle shove out.

Keefer stoked the fire and added wood. He looked at Jim Temple and said, "What the hell do you suppose happened?" The hands were on the back porch, waiting. "You might as well go back to bed," Keefer said and they walked across the yard. He filled the coffee pot and put it on the stove. "You don't suppose she walked all the way out here, do you?"

Lotte came out of the bedroom. "Pa, would you heat some water for a bath?"

"A bath?"

She frowned. "If you argue with me—"

"I'll get the water," Temple said and picked up two large oaken buckets. He went to the well, filled them, then poured them into a large copper boiler Keefer had put on the stove. The washtub was out back, hanging from a nail and he brought that to Lotte and she lugged it into the bedroom.

When the water was ready she came and got it, dipping in a bucket at a time, and Keefer and Temple smoked and drank coffee and waited and finally they came out. Martha Ivers had on one of Lotte's robes; it was a bit small for her and hit her almost at the knees.

Temple poured her some coffee and handed her into a chair; she looked at him and smiled and said, "I've really made a mess of things, Jim. I'm sorry."

"Why don't you tell us about it?" Keefer said.

Lotte brought her coffee to the table; she sat on Temple's right, crowding her chair in between Temple and her father so she could look at Martha Ivers.

"Jim, Franklin has sold you out." She let that soak in a moment, then told them about what went on in Lon Barrett's suite.

Jim Temple said, "Martha, you're goin' to marry Lon."

She shook her head. "No, I'm not now. I made up my mind to that before I left the hotel. He tried to explain to me that it was a bad thing and that he didn't like to do it, but he did it anyway, Jim. I just can't buy that." She paused to drink some of her coffee. "You knew that I didn't love Lon, but then, he didn't love me either. My mother always wanted me to marry well and the fact that I respected Lon, liked him, is really the downfall of it all because if I'd loved him, I'd not be here. He made me lose the only thing I had for him "

Tom Keefer watched her carefully and spoke with his characteristic bluntness. "It appears, from what you say, that he wasn't bein' offered a lot either."

"Yes, I suppose you'd think that. But I've been honest with him right along. He told me what he wanted in a woman: beauty, grace, and one no other man had slept with, and he didn't intend to take any woman's word for it either." She folded her hands and looked at them. "He's a man who likes terms and understands them. But I couldn't do this, Jim. It makes everything all wrong." She reached and touched Jim Temple's hand. "What shall I do? I'll have to tell him what I've done."

"Not just yet," Temple said. "First thing, I've got to get you back to town before he finds out you've gone. Tom, could I have the loan of your buggy?"

"Sure thing."

"I want to use your phone too," Temple said. "Martha, you keep your mouth shut. Don't let on to Lon what you've done. I think he's put his foot into somethin' this time." He got up and went to the hallway to ring the operator. He asked for Judge Hanlon's house. After a time a sleepy, irritable voice answered. Temple said: "Your honor, this is Sergeant Jim Temple. Sorry to get you out of bed. What's that? Yessir, I do think they're a contraption. Yessir. What I called about was something that my investigation turned up regarding the Adams brothers' trial that's on your calendar. No, sir, I'm not tryin' to try the case over the phone. Judge, there's been collusion between counsel in this matter. What's that, sir? Well, I figure on lettin' it prove itself. First off, counsel for defense is going to waive jury trial. Then he's goin' to change the plea to guilty of robbery and ask to see you in chambers with the prosecutor. The prosecutor will stipulate to the plea and ask you to hand out a minimum sentence and throw the murder charge out of court. If it happens like that, your honor, you'll know damned good and well I've proved collusion. What's that, sir? How do I know? I've got a witness to it, ready to swear in court." He listened while the judge talked, nodding in agreement. "Yessir, I'll do that. Goodnight, sir." He hung the phone and went back to the kitchen.

Lotte was sitting by herself and they went out to the back porch. "Martha's dressing," she said and crossed her arms. "She gave up a lot tonight."

"Yes. But maybe it'll work out."

"You really don't think that," she said. "Jim, she's decided. She doesn't want him now. I hope she finds out what she does want." She leaned her head against his shoulder. "Maybe I should have been jealous, the way she came to you. I know what she thinks. She'd have you in a minute, Jim."

"Aw, go on."

"I'm right and you know it."

Tom Keefer led the team and buggy from the barn and then Martha Ivers came out; Temple handed her into the rig and Lotte went in for a light robe to put around her legs because her skirt was wet. "I'd check with the doctor tomorrow," she said, then stepped back.

Temple drove out of the yard, stopping only to open and close the gate and Martha Ivers clung to a silence for a time. Then Temple said, "Did you hurt yourself somehow?" She nodded and he waited for her to say something, but she didn't so he let it go.

"Martha, can you go on pretending a little longer?"

"If I have to," she said.

"I talked to the judge and I—"

"—I heard you. Yes, I can keep it from Lon. But when he has to know, I want to tell him."

"Now you don't have to do that."

"I want to. I really mean that." She touched his arm, then quickly let go. "I like Lotte, Jim. You'll be very happy with her." She stopped talking again and he didn't pay much attention to it until he realized that she was crying.

He stopped the buggy and wrapped the reins around the whip. "I'll bet you don't do that often," he said.

"Cry?" She wiped her hand over her eyes. "Not very often. Then it's a darned flood. That's a silly woman for you."

"You can talk to me, you know."

"Yes, I know, and if I start talking I'll say too much, say things I don't have a right to say, and things that are better left unsaid. Go on, Jim. Take me back. I won't bawl any more."

"You ought to if you think it helps."

She shook her head and he drove on. "I'm just a fool. I thought I could have the things I wanted."

"What did you want?"

"The things I can't have," she said softly. "You for one."

"Oh, now hell, you're wrong about me," Temple said. "Even Lotte's lettin' herself in for a lot. I'm like the wind blowin', Martha; I'd track a lot of dust into anyone's life, and sooner or later one just gets tired of sweepin'."

"I wouldn't. She won't either. Jim, if she ever turns you down, will you think of me?"

"Don't sound like you're goin' to stand in line," he said flatly.

"But I would. I guess I am."

There was no more talk because he wanted it that way; when they reached town he turned into the alley behind the hotel, handed her down and saw her to the top of the stairs. The door was unlocked and he had a look up and down the hall before letting her go in. Then, before he could stop her, she put her hands to his face, kissed him, and ducked inside.

He stood there for a moment, then went down the stairs and got into the rig. The alley was too close and too littered to risk backing out so he drove on, turned when he reached the end and came out on the main drag. There was a light on at the jail and on impulse he drove over, thinking that if Hub Riley was alone he might throw a scare in him.

But when he stopped, the door opened and Harry Randall stepped out. "Been lookin' for you since ten o'clock," Randall said. He came up to the off wheel and stood close, talking in a very soft voice. "I've been doin' what you said, Jim. I've been watchin' the Wallace house." He turned his head and looked both ways to make sure no one was around. "He has a regular visitor."

"Who?"

"Guess."

"Oh, for Christ's sake, Harry, it's too late for guessing games."

"Fred Almquist's daughter. It's a fact. She's been goin' there ever' chance she gets. Went there tonight and stayed nearly three hours. As soon as Fred went to the hotel, here she come down the back streets. Let herself in the back door just as at home as you please. I think she's carryin' on with young Ken."

"Was his mother home?"

"Yeah, for awhile. She went shoppin' for better than an hour." He took off his hat and slapped his bald head. "I don't think it's right, two young people bein' alone like that. People will find out and talk."

"Well, you keep it to yourself. Where's Hub Riley?"

"Oh, he goes in his hole after sundown," Randall said. "He's makin' out big now with Thelma Scanlon. That woman'll take up with anybody." He looked at Temple as though he had just thought of something. "What the devil are you doin' in town so late? Everything's closed up."

"Then go on back to bed," Temple said. "I'm goin' over to Thelma's place. What Hub needs is a little excitement."

"You be careful," Randall warned. "That man's half rattlesnake."

CHAPTER
ELEVEN

"Fred, you're drinking too damned much," Lon Barrett said. He was sitting in Almquist's parlor and the shades were drawn and the house was quiet except for the hall clock chiming one-thirty.

Almquist was raising his glass; he stopped, looked at Barrett, then put it down. "I'm beginning to—"

"You're beginning to come apart at the seams," Barrett said gently. "Now, Fred, I want you to get ahold of yourself. Do you understand? There's just nothing to worry about. I tell you that because they can't prove anything at all." He burrowed deeper in the comfortable chair. "Oh, there may be some talk, but that can't hurt you, Fred. Besides, you can always announce that you've managed to negotiate a loan and will open the bank to pay the depositors in full." He spread his hands. "Sixty percent will withdraw, but then you'll have the insurance."

"I don't want to do that."

"Naturally, because you'd rather have a big cut than a little one. But I'll tell you what to do, Fred. You keep that in mind."

"Of course, Lon. I didn't mean—"

"I know what you meant," Barrett said gently. "However, you'd be much safer if Riley was out of the way. I think we ought to work on that, Fred, and not waste much time over it."

"Kill him? Damn it, didn't Morgan raise enough stink?" He picked up his glass and tossed off the drink, then made a face. "Everything was going smoothly until Morgan got a knife stuck in him."

"That's why I say we must get rid of Riley. Who else could possibly testify against you?"

Almquist looked at him a long moment. "Lon, I'm a banker, not a—you can't expect me to—kill anyone."

"Are you afraid of Riley?"

"Hell yes, I'm afraid of him. Why shouldn't I be?" He sat down and wiped a hand across his face. "Lon, I'd rather wait and see how this comes out." He waved his hand aimlessly. "I know there are a lot of newspaper people here for the trial; we're getting a lot more attention than we figured, but I'd still rather wait."

"And *I* wouldn't," Barrett said flatly. He got up and buttoned his coat. "We have about six days before this comes to trial. Be working on it." He reached out and tapped Almquist on the chest with his finger. "And don't hire it done."

"You can't leave me with a thing like that," Almquist said, taking hold of Barrett's lapels. "Lon, we've worked together a long time and this wasn't part of it."

"Now it is," Barrett said and knocked the man's hands aside. "What the hell, Fred, it can't all be easy money. Sometimes you have to bend down and pick it up."

"You never bend down." He drew back. "I won't do it. Jail scares me a lot less than the hangman, Lon. I just won't do it. I'd rather call in all the outstanding notes I hold and disperse what assets remain. By God, as far as these people are concerned, I'm still the banker."

"All right, all right," Barrett said gently, patting Almquist on the chest. "Don't panic, Fred. We'll trust to luck a little longer." He gnawed on his cold cigar. "That's not a bad idea, dispersing some of the assets. Why don't you do that? It'll ease some of the bad feeling in town, and it'll give you something to do to keep your mind off your troubles." He patted Almquist again. "Give the story out to the papers in the morning. It'll make good copy. Money always does."

Almquist nodded but his worry was not eased. "I wish we hadn't done this, Lon. It was too close, two years. That's much too close."

"Now I didn't think so, and I'm the one who decides," Barrett said. "Good night, Fred. And try to sleep. You look like hell."

He stepped out the door and closed it quietly after him. Then Almquist turned out the lights and went slowly up the stairs to his room. His wife was snoring indelicately and down the hall, the

186

door of his daughter's room was slightly ajar. He moved to close it, then glanced inside; the bed had not been slept in at all and he turned on the light and looked around. The closet door was open and he saw at a glance that many of her clothes and a large leather suitcase was gone.

For a moment he didn't know what to do; his first impulse was to wake his wife, then he decided not to do that; she would only cry and carry on and confuse him. Almquist turned off the light and gently closed the door. She was gone and he was not surprised because he never knew what she was going to do next; he didn't understand her and she had never really talked to him, not in the last few years anyway; he had lost contact with her and it really hadn't seemed important to him to pick it up.

Slowly he went back to his own room and sat on the edge of the bed and unlaced his shoes. His wife stirred but did not wake up and he was glad of that because she'd want to ask questions and he was in no mood for answering them.

Jim Temple left the buggy parked by the jail and walked three blocks over to a poor section of town where the houses were small and unpainted; Thelma Scanlon's place was a block beyond, an old two-story house of many rooms, which she put to good use.

The street was very dark for it was a moonless

night and the trees made ink of every shadow. He heard a gate squeak gently and a whispered word and he stopped to listen. Then he saw ahead two shadows merge and part and start along the walk. They carried suitcases and they saw him standing there and the girl gasped and put her hand over her mouth.

"What's goin' on?" Temple asked, stepping close to identify them.

"Oh, please be quiet," the girl said.

Temple struck a match for an instant, then whipped it out; he recognized Ken Wallace and Gena Almquist. "What are you two up to?"

"Please," Gena said, "can't we move away from the house?"

"Let's walk back toward the jail," Temple said. When they reached the corner he looked at them. "Running away?"

"We're leaving," Ken said. "I don't call that running away."

"What I call leavin' is in broad daylight," Jim Temple pointed out. "Runnin' away is done at two o'clock in the morning. Now you ought to get clear on that."

"Mr. Temple, everyone isn't as brave as you," Gena said. "But that doesn't mean they want a thing less."

"It does seem that you have a point there," he admitted. When they reached the jail, he stopped. "No one's inside but the constable and the

Adams brothers, and they're sleeping. You want to come in for some coffee? How were you going to get out of town?"

"The northbound freight," Ken Wallace said. "I know the brakie and he'll let me ride in the caboose." He stepped inside and looked around. "I've never been in a jail before. Not even in the office."

Harry Randall was snoring away in the side room and Temple quietly closed the door so they wouldn't wake him; he poured some lukewarm coffee and passed the canned milk and sugar. Then he sat on the desk and looked at them, smiling a little. "You think it ain't brave to take off like this in a big, rough world? What will you do for a livin', Ken?"

"Oh, clerk in a store, or get another job in a bank. I'm good with figures and I can do almost any kind of office work." He looked seriously at Jim Temple. "Could I ask a favor?"

"Think you have one comin'?"

"No, but it isn't for me."

"Go ahead."

"Well, Gena and I would like to talk to the Adams brothers."

Temple thought about it. "You want me to wake 'em up so you can talk to 'em? All right, come on." He led the way back through the cell blocks. There was a small lamp hanging from the wires, casting a gloomy light in the corridor. He stopped by the door and shook it slightly and Woody Adams came awake; he nudged his brothers and they sat up.

"Got a couple of people here who want to talk to you," Temple said.

"This ain't exactly the social hour," Woody said.

"It sure ain't," Otis agreed. "Wakin' a man up at this hour could rob the provocative bloom from his cheeks."

"Where'd you learn a word like that?" Woody wanted to know. "I'd rather hear a man swear."

Ken Wallace said, "Have any of you ever seen me before?"

They studied him carefully then shook their heads. "Nope," Woody admitted. "We ain't. Don't tell me we missed somethin'?"

"This is Ken Wallace, the clerk in the bank who was hit on the head during the robbery," Temple explained. "Have you ever seen them before, Ken?"

"No, and that's the truth."

Gena Almquist stepped up and gripped the bars as though she intended to tear the door away and free them. "I know you didn't do it," she said. "I wish I could help you."

"Well, little girl, it's kind of been a help, just you sayin' it," Woody Adams said. "You know, you sit in here awhile and pretty soon you get to thinkin'—well, it's nice of you to say it." He turned and went back to his cot and Temple touched Wallace on the arm and took them back to the office.

He sat on the edge of the desk and said, "It's kind of a shame, you leavin', Ken. I mean, you could swear in court that you'd never seen 'em before and it would have some weight. But I guess a man's got to think of himself first, doesn't he?"

"I'm coming back for the trial," Wallace said, surprised to find Temple thinking otherwise. "We've got ten days. That's time enough to get settled some place. I'll be back, Jim. That's a promise."

He nodded and looked from one to the other. "I don't suppose either of you bothered to say good-bye at home."

"Good-bye to what?" Gena said. "We'd better go if we're going to catch the train, Ken."

"I'll drive you in the buggy," Temple said and went outside with them. He put their suitcases in back, boosted Gena to the seat, then turned right down the main street and drove through town to the depot.

The freight was making up and Wallace took the suitcases into the caboose, then came back to Temple, who waited by the buggy. Gena was in front of the station, sitting on one of the benches.

"There's none of us has a crystal ball," Jim Temple said, unbuttoning his shirt pocket. He palmed the .41 derringer and then slipped it into

Ken Wallace's coat pocket. "A man ought to be able to protect a woman, or himself, if he has to. I guess you've figured out who really robbed the bank; you're not stupid."

"Mr. Almquist. It couldn't be any other way."

"That's right, but he didn't conk you on the head. So if you've figured that out, you may figure out who smells of bay rum and sweat all the time." He smiled at the surprised expression on Wallace's face. "When you get another sniff, that'll tell you that someone figures you weren't hit hard enough and that little two-shot is goin' to feel mighty comfortable."

"Who cold decked me, Mr. Temple? I did get a whiff just before all the lights went out. Do you know?"

"An educated guess," Temple said, "but I'd put Hub Riley high on the list. Let me put it this way: if you see Hub Riley, wherever you go, figure that he's after you." He slapped the young man on the shoulder. "Send me a piece of the wedding cake, Ken."

"By golly, I'll do that."

Carl Yoder came around the corner of the depot, lantern in hand. "Let's go, Ken. Howdy, Jim."

"Take care of 'em," Temple said.

"Far's Enid. That's end of line for me."

Temple did not wait until the freight pulled out; he heard it huffing out of the yard as he drove back toward the jail, and then he sat in the buggy for a time, thinking, wishing he could find one thing on which to base a move. But he couldn't move against Hub Riley, not on suspicion, and he couldn't openly accuse Fred Almquist without proof. It filled Jim Temple with a sense of failure, to be able to do nothing; he'd been sent there to make a big noise and he wasn't doing it and he wasn't sure how he was going to explain that to Captain Rickert.

Then there was the stolen money. The Adams boys would be accused of hiding it some place, but of course they never had it although Lon Barrett would do his damndest to make the judge believe they'd hid it.

Jim Temple went over the possibilities very carefully. He was sure that Hub Riley had belted young Wallace on the skull, so Hub could have taken the money. But that didn't seem too likely, to Temple's way of thinking. Almquist wouldn't trust Riley with sixteen thousand dollars.

So Hub didn't take the money.

That left Almquist, who probably carried it home that evening in a briefcase or under his coat. Still, a man had to consider Fred Almquist carefully before deciding that was the way it was. Almquist wouldn't tell his wife that he was robbing his own bank, so it didn't seem likely that he took the money home with him.

It was Jim Temple's opinion that the money never left the bank at all, and the more he considered it, the more logical it became. Almquist closed the bank immediately after the robbery, and there would be no audit of the books until the insurance investigator came to settle the claim, and that would take time because they'd wait for the local law to investigate.

The money could lay in the vault or the desk drawer and no one would ever suspect it, and later, before the investigators arrived, Almquist could remove it a bit at a time or all at once, which ever suited him best.

Harry Randall came out of the jail then and relieved himself in the bushes by the steps and Temple said, "Can't you go out back?"

This startled Randall and he splashed on himself and swore. "What the hell you doin' sittin' out here?"

"Waitin' for you to do that," Temple said, letting the darkness hide his smile. "That's against the state law, you know. If that bush dies now that'll be defacin' a public building. Ten days or ten dollars."

"Oh, go to hell," Randall said and started back inside. He changed his mind and sat down on the steps. "Jim, I just don't know how to take you sometimes. Don't anything excite you?"

"I like to look at rain clouds." He rolled a cigaret and struck a match. "Hub Riley don't sleep much in the jail, does he? You suppose his conscience is botherin' him?"

"Don't think he's got one."

"Sure would be nice if Miles Morgan had a ghost to come back and haunt Riley." He chuckled.

"If you're thinkin' of me puttin' a sheet over my head, forget it," Randall said and scratched his bald head. "You didn't go over to Thelma's?"

"Got sidetracked."

"I hear she's got a Chinee girl in there who's a lulu."

"Your wife know you go in Thelma's place?"

"God, no."

"They tell me there's nothin' harder for a married man to do than explain where he got a dose. I'd think about that, Harry. Your wife may not be as excitin' as the Chinese girl, but there's been many a sweet tune played on an old fiddle."

Randall laughed without humor. "Jim, if I'd had you to guide me in my youth, I may have amounted to somethin'." He slapped his knees and got up. "Sit out here if you want to. I'm goin' in and get some more sleep."

After the constable closed the door, Jim Temple got down from the rig and walked two blocks down the dark and quiet main street. Above the drugstore, light came through a pair of windows and he went up the stairs and stepped into the telephone company switchboard office.

The operator was dozing in a leather chair; she came awake at the slight sound of the door closing. "Oh, you startled me." She was forty some, a little prim and bony, the kind of a woman who looked like she'd protected her virtue when she should have yielded and got a husband. "No one is allowed in here, Mr. Temple. You know the company rules."

"No I don't," he said, sitting down. "I want to make a call to Captain George Rickert, Laredo, and after you get all the plugs put in the right holes, I want you to go downstairs for a stroll."

"Why, I couldn't do that!"

"Lady, what I've got to say to the captain I don't even want the Lord to overhear. Now you've got nothin' against savin' a man from hangin', have you?" He smiled and reached out and patted her arm. "Now come on, stick in the right plugs."

"Jim Temple, I'm liable to get fired for this."

"No you won't, and I'll promise you that."

"Well—" She sat down at the switchboard and made connections, talking to operators on down the line, then she handed him her headset. "He's mad and I don't blame him." She went out, her hard heels clicking on the stairs.

"Hello, Captain? Sergeant Temple here."

"Do you know what the hell time it is?"

Temple winced and pulled the headset away from his ear, then explained the purpose of the call. He talked for five minutes and didn't waste words, then he waited a moment while Rickert thought it over.

"Jim, the insurance investigators aren't going to call for an audit until he's filed a claim with them. Technically there hasn't been a robbery as far as they're concerned. So that doesn't help you much."

"Captain, I've got to get into that bank. How about a court order?"

"Not without cause. I don't think the judge would issue one without proof, and all you have is a strong hunch."

"Break in some night, sir?"

"Don't say that word! Don't even think it. Hold on a minute and let me think."

"A fire, captain?"

"Shut up." There was a moment when the wires hummed. "Why don't you get Almquist to open it for you?"

"How?"

"Think of something."

"Well, sir, I called you because you are my captain, my leader, and I look up to you and respect you and—"

"Aw, cut it out; you'll have me sobbing in a moment," Rickert said. "I'm serious, Temple. Tell him you want to make another physical examination of the premises. He can't legally refuse that, and if he does, the judge will be glad to give you an order. Once you get inside, take your time, but figure out a way to get back in, especially without him knowing it. Then, in the company of a reliable witness, find the money, and pray that it's there, because if you're caught and it's not there—"

"Yes, sir. If I find the money, should I remove it?"

"God, that would throw him in a panic, wouldn't it? I don't want to give you an answer, Jim. Play it by ear; you're makin' good music."

"It seems like I'm not gettin' anywhere, Captain."

"I disagree, Jim. You keep it up. And you keep those three boys from getting hung, you hear?"

"Yes, sir. I'll sure do that if I have to break 'em out of jail myself. Sir? Did you slap your forehead, Captain?"

"Next time, call me when it's daylight." He clicked the receiver and Temple opened the window and whistled for the operator to come back and take out the plugs. She came up the stairs and into the room shaking her head.

"You're a sweetheart," Temple said.

She smiled. "Fifteen years ago I'd have considered that a proposal."

"Maybe I'd have meant it that way," Temple said and left the office, whistling softly as he went down the stairs. He wasn't sure what made him feel so happy, but he supposed it was the assurance Rickert had given him that he wasn't botching his first assignment. Or it could be that he was going to be doing something, making a move in this game instead of evaluating the moves the others were making.

He was tired now and he went to the hotel and his room and unlocked his door and the moment he pushed it open part way he felt the warning hit him and he slammed his weight against the door, sending it back crashing it full force into Hub Riley.

It staggered the sheriff and he cursed and clutched his head and there was just enough light coming through the window for Temple to see the man, knife in hand, shaking his head, trying to get his bearings.

Temple axed a blow to Riley's face and ducked the knife although he felt the tip of it bite into the flesh of his shoulder and pass on, leaving a shallow bleeding gash. He fended the knife, grabbed the wrist, and twisted, at the same time hitting Riley again in the face and wringing a grunt from him.

The knife fell to the floor and Temple locked an arm around Riley's neck, half strangling him with the power of the grip. He squeezed and twisted and dragged Riley from the room and down the hall and Riley beat his fists against Temple's back and head but Riley was hurting and he didn't have enough power left to get loose.

Freeing one hand just enough to open the back door leading to the stairway, Temple forced the man through and kicked the door shut, then stood on the small porch and battered Riley's face with his fist, grunting with the effort each time he hit the man.

The strength seemed to leave Riley's legs and he sagged but still Jim Temple hit him until there was no resistance in the man at all. He propped him against the wall, tore the badge from his shirt and threw it down the alley. Then he gave Riley a shove and sent him cascading, bouncing, somersaulting down the stairs, bouncing against the railing posts until he neared the bottom, where he slipped off and fell ten feet, crashing through some stacked wooden crates.

Jim Temple stood a moment, breathing deeply, quieting the anger that had made him do this, then he opened the door and stepped into the hallway. A man had his head out and Temple said, "Some drunk fell down the steps."

"Sounded like a fight," the man said.

"A drunk can sound like a herd of buffalo sometimes."

"That's a fact," the man said and closed the door.

In his room, Temple turned on the light and picked up Hub Riley's folding jackknife; it had a blade long enough to skewer a shoat and he folded it and put it in his hip pocket.

He took off his shirt and peeled down his underwear and looked at the cut on his shoulder. It wasn't bad but he intended to see a doctor and get it cleaned and dressed. Likely a couple of stitches would close it.

Then he washed and undressed and before he settled down on the bed he opened the window wide. It had hit him, the odor of sweat and bay rum, like an ax because he'd come from fresh air and Riley had been in the room for at least an hour.

And it had been all the warning Temple had needed.

He supposed it had been a bit of luck, talking about the way Riley always smelled, unwashed, then covering the stink with bay rum; that had made him react without wasting time figuring it out. And he wasn't sure what he should do, thank Ken Wallace or tell Riley to take a bath.

Temple was sure of one thing: if Riley ever tried anything like that again, he wouldn't need another bath.

CHAPTER
TWELVE

Jim Temple was having his breakfast in the hotel dining room when Harry Randall hurried in and hauled himself down in a chair. "Did you hear the news? Some fellas found Hub Riley staggerin' around in an alley down the street less than twenty minutes ago."

"Drunk?"

"No, someone had beaten the livin' bejasus out of him. He's over at Doc Potter's place right now." Randall grinned hugely. "Oh, boy, I'd like to have seen that. Oh, boy, I really would." He washed his hands together briskly. "Oh, golllll-eeeeee, that must have been somethin'. And it couldn't happen to a nicer guy."

"Don't sound so glum about it," Temple said, forcing back his smile. "He may recover."

"Glum? Hell, I'm—aw, you're kiddin' me again. Well, I better get home. The old lady gets on the warpath easy enough."

"Thanks for tellin' me, Harry," Temple said. "You want some breakfast?"

"No, I always eat at home." He scurried out of the dining room and Jim Temple finished his meal, feeling very pleased with himself. He was happy to hear that the tumble down the stairs hadn't been fatal; at the time he had sent Riley on his flight he hadn't cared one way or another. But he was glad Riley was alive.

After he paid his bill, Temple walked two doors down to the stairs leading up to Doctor Adamo Chianti's office; he went into the waiting room and sat down. Through the door he could hear the soft run of Chianti's voice; he had an early patient and Temple picked up a magazine and began to read.

Twenty minutes later the door opened and Martha Ivers stepped out; Chianti was with her, a gnome of a man with a waxed mustache and good white teeth backed by a wide smile.

"How are you, Jeem?" he said, his accent thick.

"Pretty good," Temple said. "What are you doin' here, Martha?"

Chianti looked from one to the other. "You two are acquaint?" He shrugged; it was none of his business. "I advise rest, Senorita. And no more horseback riding." He opened the door for her and bowed; his manner was very continental, and when he appeared on the street it was always in pin-stripe trousers, hat, gloves, cane. And in addition, Temple considered him the best doctor in north Texas.

Martha turned before the door closed. "Jim, call on me today."

"I'll try," he promised, then the door shut and she went down the stairs.

"I'd be obliged if you'd do a little needle work on me, Doc," Temple said. He stepped into Chianti's office and took off his shirt and dropped the shoulder of his underwear. Chianti studied the cut, making little chirping, whistling noises, then he washed it carefully and put a bandage on it and a wide piece of tape.

"It will heal best if left undisturbed," he said, regarding Temple seriously. "You—wouldn't care to tell me where you got this, would you?" He clapped his hands together. "Already I heard that my colleague down the street had a patient in serious condition. This patient is known to carry a large knife. You do not find my addition of interest?"

"You wouldn't believe me if I told you I cut this shaving?"

"Jeem, I would not infer that you would lie to me, much the same as I would not suggest that my other patient resorted to a falsehood." He shook his first and let an anger show in the livid hue of his complexion. "Were I not a man of position, I'd horsewhip a man."

"You know, Adamo, I don't understand half the things you say."

He laughed and made an explosive sound with his lips. "Half of the time I do not understand myself. Now go. I will have many patients today and grow rich and return to Italy and keep a woman." He laughed and took Temple by the arm and steered him out into the waiting room. "For this profound advice I will not charge."

"Now you'll never get rich that way."

Chianti shrugged and made a wry face and Temple went down the stairs, buttoning his shirt. The sun was good and strong and promised a day of steady heat; he turned down the street toward Fred Almquist's house and when he got there he knocked for several minutes before Mrs. Almquist came to the door.

Her eyes were puffed and red-rimmed; they looked like they were ready to bleed. She kept a handkerchief pressed to her mouth and stepped back, wordlessly ushering him inside. Fred Almquist was pacing up and down the parlor; he looked around and snapped, "What do you want, Temple? Can't you see there's grief in this house?"

"What'd you do, lose a dime?"

Mrs. Almquist sobbed and ran to woman's retreat, the kitchen.

"Now see what you've done," Almquist said. "What is it you want, Temple?" He waved his hand absently. "Our daughter has run away from home. At a time like this do you think it's proper to bother a man?"

"Her and Wallace went to Enid, Oklahoma, to get married," Temple said casually, all the time watching Almquist's expression, particularly his eyes.

He made a good show of shock and outrage, but it wasn't genuine and Temple knew it. "Why, she's just a baby, a little girl."

"She's eighteen and pretty darned well filled out, Fred."

"How do you know where she is?" Almquist asked.

"Oh, I saw 'em off on the northbound freight last night." He ran his fingers through his hair. "Say, Fred, I want to have another look around the bank. Just in case there's some physical evidence I've overlooked. You know, I never did get around to a real thorough examination and—"

"Surely it can wait," Almquist suggested.

" 'Fraid it can't."

"Ohgoddamnitallright," Almquist said testily. "I want to talk to my wife a minute though." He went into the kitchen and a moment later her wail came through the house like a muted fire siren. Temple walked around the room, looking at the drapes and the pictures in the ornate frames; he punched furniture and lifted vases and even peeked into a few rosewood boxes lying about.

Then Almquist came back, got his hat and they went out together. At the bank, while he fumbled with his keys, Temple leaned against the brick wall; the sun was already warming them. Then he stepped inside and Almquist closed and locked the door; there was a deadbolt on the inside that he turned.

"Is the back door locked the same way?" Temple asked, notebook and pencil ready to write down the answers.

"Yes. They're really the best locks," Almquist said. "To open one from the outside you'd have to saw the bolt in two and they're tough steel. And too, you can tell at a glance whether or not the door is locked." He pointed. "The knob is a bar and when it's horizontal, the bolt is home."

"Very interesting," Temple said and examined the lock. The bar handle was held on by a screw and he guessed set on a squared shaft.

He asked questions, dozens of them: How thick were the walls? The bars on the windows? Were the locks on the tellers' drawers substantial?

Temple pestered Almquist with questions and painstakingly put down the answers, filling several pages in the notebook and gradually wearing Almquist's patience to a frazzle.

Could he look in the vault?

It took Almquist ten minutes to open it and Temple nearly an hour to finish his ohing and ahing about the construction. After two hours of this, Almquist was getting snappy, and suddenly he said, "There's no more to see in here," and ushered Temple out of the vault and closed it, spinning the lock. "Look, I can't fool around here all day. Besides, it's getting hot in here. I'm going to step over to Ben Perch's place for a beer. Will you please try and be through in here by the time I get back?"

He went out, slamming the door and Temple moved to the back of the bank, taking Hub Riley's snap blade from his hip pocket. He had no trouble unscrewing the screw that held the deadbolt handle, but before taking it off, he opened the bolt, then reset the handle a quarter of a turn so that it looked like it was closed.

When Almquist came back Temple was pacing off the front of the room; this took some time and he wrote it all down, then once more made Almquist show him where he had stood and where Wallace had been standing and where the bandits stood.

All this was paced off and put down.

"Are—you—finished?" Almquist said, spacing the words.

"Yes, I am, and you've been very cooperative about this, Fred. I want to thank you for it."

"To hell with that," he snapped. "I've got business of my own to attend to, family business. I'm going to have a warrant sworn out against Ken Wallace and have Riley serve it. No young —tomcat is going to steal my daughter and get away with it." He opened the door, flung it wide. "Now, Temple, if you please."

"Sure, Fred. I hated to put you out like this. That's the truth." Almquist was locking the door, not paying any attention to Temple at all and he just walked away, leaving Temple standing there, talking to himself.

Temple watched him stomp on down the street, and he let a small smile build up the corners of his lips. Then he went to the small barn behind the jail, got Tom Keefer's buggy and drove out of town. He felt pretty good about the whole thing now and whistled while he drove along. Fred Almquist had been very nice, as nice as any man could be; Temple thought so because Almquist had practically told him where he kept his money.

Lotte was beating rugs when Temple put up the team; he came over, took the beater away from her and worked up a good sweat while she sat on the sawhorse and watched him. When he finished, she said, "By golly, I've got to hand it to you—you're not lazy." She cocked her head to one side and regarded him, her expression amused. "You didn't have any trouble getting home last night, did you?"

"Nope."

"I really took a chance. She's the kind of a woman who could make a man leave home and mother."

"So are you."

"Am I really?" She jumped up and flung her arms around him. "Oh, I love you for saying it." Then she let go and stepped back. "Say, you never did tell me what Nora Shannon wanted the other night."

"By golly, I didn't, did I?" He kept a straight face. "I'll have to some day."

She wrinkled her nose. "Tell me now."

"Aw, not now. It'll give you somethin' to look forward to." He took out his tobacco and made a cigaret. "Where's your pa?"

"He is fixing a fence. About Nora Sha—"

"You don't have anything cold inside to drink, do you?"

"You're not going to tell me?"

He shook his head. "It wouldn't concern us, Lotte. Besides, it isn't my place to say what people tell me in confidence."

She took his arm. "Sure, Jim. I ragged you and I'm sorry."

He made a fist and caught her small nose in the crook of his little finger, and gently tweeked it. "You've got a good head, Lotte." Then he slapped the solid roundness of her bottom. "Good shape too."

"Say now, you just notice everything, don't you?" She laughed and went into the house.

Tom Keefer and the hands came in for lunch and Temple talked to him awhile by the barn. Then Keefer and the hands went back to work and Temple stretched out on the glider on the back porch and slept until supper time. Then he went to the bathhouse the hands had rigged up, took a shower, and came back to the table just as Lotte was putting out the platters.

There was just casual talk during the meal, about the weather and crops and whether or not the market prices would hold up. Then the hands excused themselves and left and the talk began to weathervane.

"Tom and I are goin' into town late tonight," Temple said. "So don't wait up for us." He looked at Lotte and found her waiting for him to go on, to explain himself. "Tom and I have some bankin' business that just can't wait."

"Yeah," Keefer said. "We're goin' to make a withdrawal."

Temple explained his theory about where the supposedly stolen money was. "Now I've been to Fred's house off and on for some years; since he's the mayor as well as the banker, I'd had business with him. I did notice that his wife really rules the roost, so it ain't likely that he took the money home with him. That leaves the bank." He described his fruitless search of the bank. "My object was to get Fred sore at me, so I fooled around and fussed and thought he'd never give up, then he went and had a beer. That gave me a chance to fix the lock on the back door. I told Fred I wanted to see the vault and he opened it up for me, showed me all the safe deposit boxes and how they worked; he wasn't hesitant about anything so I know the money ain't in there."

"Where the hell is it then?" Keefer wanted to know.

"In Ken Wallace's cashier drawer. You know Almquist has three men in the bank besides himself; two tellers and a cashier. I asked him about the drawers and he opened two for me, but not Wallace's. When I asked him about that, he told me that I was making a needless nuisance of the whole thing and that Wallace's was the same as the others. He got pretty snippy about it and since there was money in the drawers and I'd looked in, he insisted on counting it before locking them." He laughed softly. "Probably figured that would insult me real good."

"How come there was money in the drawers?" Lotte asked.

"Oh, the robbers never really clean any bank. They grab the big stuff and hit the vaults, but the cashiers always have four or five hundred or more in their drawers. And robbers rarely fool with silver, and there must have been five thousand in silver in the vault that hadn't been touched."

"How are you going to get that drawer open?" Tom Keefer asked.

"Pry it." He took out his watch. "I figure we can leave around ten o'clock. I want another witness. Do you suppose Al Shannon would meet us in town without askin' a lot of questions over the phone?"

"I'll go call him," Keefer said and left the table.

"Jim, if this doesn't work out—"

He held up his hands and waved them. "I don't

even want to think of it because you can send me tobacco and cookies at Huntsville Prison." He folded his hands and looked at them. "Lotte, the other night, Nora Shannon told me enough to take it before the judge, but I just can't bring myself to use her testimony. I just can't see her ruin herself and her father and her brothers, and it would too. So what can I do? Make someone break, that's all. That money missing ought to set Fred Almquist off."

Keefer came back and sat down. "Al will meet us by the jail at eleven."

"Fine. Tom, I'll need a couple of long screwdrivers or pry bars. And a shoebox and three or four candles."

"Got that all right."

"And I want some paper and a pen and a regular envelope."

"Lotte will get that for you." He scraped back his chair. "Think I'll get some shuteye before we leave." He gave Lotte a playful pat on the cheek and went to his room.

At a quarter to ten, Jim Temple made sure he had everything ready; he had prepared a statement, ready for signatures, and had the envelope in his pocket. The tools were on the back porch and he had saddled two horses and then Lotte went to wake her father. Keefer came out and stood on the porch.

"Will I need a gun?"

"No. Let's go." Temple put the tools in the saddlebag and they mounted and rode out. When they got to town, Temple went in on the quiet back streets where the houses were dark, shut up for the night. He came around in back of the jail and Keefer went to find Al Shannon, returning a moment later.

"What the hell's goin' on?" Shannon asked and Temple took five minutes to explain it to him. The whole idea pleased Shannon and they left their horses there and circled afoot to the alley behind the bank.

Keefer carried the tools and Temple tried the door; it opened under his hand and they stepped inside. Temple then changed the handle back to the original position and locked the door. With the shades drawn, the bank was like the inside of a thick sack and they moved carefully, Temple leading them, and hunkered down behind Ken Wallace's cage.

By feel, Temple located the drawer and slipped the blade of a heavy screwdriver in it, adding pressure until the wood groaned and creaked. He would allow no one else to touch anything or help in any way. Then he inserted the other screwdriver, bore down and felt the wood give and the drawer came open.

He lit a candle and made Shannon hold it, cupping his hand around the flame. Temple didn't think that the light could be seen from the street, but he wanted to take no chances. The money was there, crowded in the back of the drawer; he took the whole drawer out and laid it on the floor, then removed the lid off the shoebox and transferred the money, not allowing either of them to touch it, but insisting that they count it carefully.

The money was all there and Temple put the lid on the shoebox, then patiently melted the candle, and another, and sealed the lid tightly. He took the letter he had prepared, read it, and they each signed it, using the bank's pen and ink. This was also sealed to the box with wax, then they picked up the burned matches and candle stubs and tools and left the drawer on the floor.

Before leaving, Temple went to the front door and gently turned the bolt back so that it was open, then they went out the back way and walked the length of the alley to the dark side street. All the time Temple insisted that Al Shannon carry one end of the box and Tom Keefer the other, carrying it between them as though it were heavy.

There was a light on in Judge Hanlon's parlor and he answered Temple's knock. They stepped inside and Hanlon said, "This is unexpected. Good evening, Tom, Al. What can I do for you gentlemen? My wife is out or I'd offer you something."

They shook their heads and waved their hands and murmured that it was all right; they couldn't stay anyway. Hanlon saw the box and the way they carried it. Jim Temple said, "Judge, I have a request to make that may sound unusual to you, but you'd be servin' the cause of justice if you went along with it."

"Well, I certainly won't refuse to do that," Hanlon admitted.

"I want to turn this box and the contents over to you, sir," Temple said. "As you can see, it is sealed and the letter is sealed to the lid. It contains important evidence. Both these men know what it contains because they saw me put it there. And they watched me seal the box and since that moment, they have not let it out of their hands."

"You want me to keep it?"

"Yes, sir, and say nothing to anyone that you have it."

"All right," Hanlon said and took the box.

"There's one more thing, your honor. I would like to have a meeting called in your chambers for day after tomorrow. One o'clock ought to do nicely. I'd like Fred Almquist there, and Senator Barrett and Stanley Franklin. I want the three Adams brothers, Tom and Al here, and Sheriff Riley."

"He's out of town, Temple."

"Did you issue a warrant?"

"No, the whole thing was ridiculous. But he went anyway."

"I see," Temple said, frowning.

"But there are some things I don't see," Hanlon admitted. "Just what is it you intend to do, Temple?"

"I'm goin' to prove who robbed the bank, and how it was done."

"Well now, I think that's an ambitious undertaking. Would you like it if I invited these men independently, so that they weren't aware that anyone beside themselves—"

"Yes, sir, that'd be just fine."

Hanlon tapped the box with his fingers. "I trust we'll open this then?"

"Yes."

"And we'll all be surprised?"

"We sure will be, judge."

"My, I can hardly wait."

They said goodnight and walked as far as the front gate; Temple showed a new graveness. "I've got to get to the telegraph office. That damned Riley's goin' to kill Wallace sure as hell."

"He wouldn't dare do that," Shannon said.

"The hell he wouldn't," Keefer said. "He's goin' to bring back a man's daughter and if he just accidentally had to shoot Wallace doin' it, what jury do you think would convict him? Hell, I can just hear his lawyer spoutin' off about the glory and virtue of Texas womanhood." He slapped Temple on the arm. "You go on. Figure out how to save Wallace."

"I've got a six-shooter in my saddlebag," Shannon said. "Riley would never be lookin' for me. If I could catch the late freight out I might—"

"Yeah, and you might get yourself killed too,"

Keefer said. "You're gettin' old, Al. And you ain't mean like Riley. You'd give him an even break no matter what and that'd be all that man would need to do you in."

"Tom's right. Stay here. Riley will come back. There's no need gettin' him suspicious."

"Well, you've got good sense, Jim," Shannon admitted. "I'm goin' home. See you day after tomorrow." He turned and walked on back toward the jail and Temple went to the telegraph office.

The operator was asleep and Temple woke him. He scribbled the wire and the operator counted it, tapping the tip of his pencil on each word:

CITY MARSHAL
ENID OKLAHOMA
IMPERATIVE YOU LOCATE NEWLYWED KENNETH WALLACE AND BRIDE TONIGHT AND SEE THAT THEY GET ON FIRST SOUTHBOUND URGENT REPLY REQUESTED

J. TEMPLE
SGT E CO
TEXAS RNGRS

"You could save fifteen cents if you cut out this wo—"

"To hell with it. Send it." He motioned to a chair by the cold stove. "All right if I sit there and wait?"

"May be a couple hours."

"I'll wait," Temple said and went over and sat down, listening to the operator clear the line, then transmit the message.

He smoked and worried and once he got up and went outside to pace, then, by his watch, an hour and eighteen minutes later, the key began to chatter and Temple went in to get his message. He grabbed the wire from the man's hand and read:

WALLACE AND WIFE DEPARTED CITY
ON ELEVEN TEN

D CANBY
U S MARSHAL

Temple laughed and wadded the paper up and threw it in the fire. The telegrapher said, "I guess that was worth waitin' for, huh?"

"Man, you just know it," Temple said and went uptown to find Tom Keefer.

He could sleep now.

CHAPTER
THIRTEEN

Harry Randall, the conscientious constable, in making his early morning rounds checking doors, found the bank door open and for a moment he just didn't know what to do about it because nothing like this had ever happened to him before.

He thought of ringing the firebell; that would get everyone out all right, but they'd be sore about it, especially the firemen. Then too, he'd have to leave the bank unguarded while he went to ring the bell, so he ruled this out.

The best thing, he decided, would be to fire his pistol and attract attention; he carried it in a flap holster in his hip pocket and had a little trouble because the brass button had turned green and stuck to the punched hole in the leather. He had not fired his pistol in eleven years and hadn't cleaned it in the last seven; he found the action so dusty and gummed that he could not pull the trigger double action so he stood there, cocking it with thumb and shooting it into the air.

His fourth shot brought heads out of upper windows. "Get the sheriff!" Randall yelled. "The bank's been busted into!"

"The sheriff's out of town," one man said.

"Then get Jim Temple! Hurry up, will you?" Randall had some cartridges in his pocket and he got them out, meaning to reload. The cartridges were worn shiny and the lead had been nicked by keys and coins and when he went to swing the cylinder out, it wouldn't budge, so he stood there, gun in hand, with two shots left, resigned to the fact that if the robbers were still in there he'd shoot twice more and then go out a hero.

From the direction of the depot, Ken Wallace and his new bride walked toward Randall; Wallace was lugging suitcases.

Wallace said, "Gosh, Mr. Randall, what's going on? I heard shooting."

"The bank's been busted into. Go on, get off the street before Fred Almquist sees you; he's too mad to just spit." He gave them a shove toward the hotel just as a crowd started to gather.

Jim Temple finally showed up; he went inside and had a look around just as brave as you please, then he came out. "Anyone gone to fetch Fred Almquist?"

A man in back raised on tiptoe and said, "I seen someone trottin' toward his house."

"There's no need for you people to be here," Temple said gently. "Why don't you all go have your breakfast and afterward maybe we'll have some news for you?"

That sounded very reasonable to them, but one man grinned and said, "Hey, Harry, what you holdin' your gun for?"

"The constable is doin' his duty, what you pay him to do," Temple said quickly. He glanced at Randall and saw the relief in the man's eyes. "You keep your pistol handy until we find out just what's goin' on here."

Fred Almquist came panting down the street, suspenders flapping; he had on neither coat nor collar and he bulled through, stared at the door ajar, then a cry of anguish burst from him and he charged into the bank. He saw the cash drawer on the floor with several hundred dollars in bills and coins still in it, and he fell to his knees, thumping them on the hard floor, and put both hands over his face.

Temple and Randall had come in and Temple closed the door, motioning for Randall to put his gun away. Then Temple walked over and said, "Looks like you had a break-in here, Fred. First off, I want you to take inventory and see what's been taken."

Almquist slowly turned his head and looked at Jim Temple, who kept his expression neutral. In Almquist's eyes there was a look Temple had never seen before, the look of a man who had lost everything and had to suffer it in silence. He was a man struck a mortal blow who could not reveal the slightest hint of his agony.

For three hours Jim Temple made Almquist

minutely check books and add up the cash remaining, made him stay there while the hot fire burned in his mind and the eighteen thousand, one hundred and eight dollars, which could not be spoken of, or alluded to, was gone.

The newspaper man wanted a story, and Jim Temple let him in; he questioned Fred Almquist and it was torture to listen to the halting answers, the mind continually swinging away and being swung back. Almquist was visibly trembling when the newspaper man left and Temple said, "Well, Fred, you ought to go home and get a drink. It don't look like anything's missin' here, but I guess the thought of bein' robbed again, so soon, has been more than you could take."

Almquist tried to speak, but just couldn't get the words out. He let Temple lead him out and steer him on a course toward home. Temple stood with Randall and they looked after the man and Randall said, "He's takin' it hard, ain't he?"

"Yeah, but he's holdin' it in real well. This has been more of a shock to him than we know, Harry." He turned and clapped the constable on the shoulder. "You handled this just fine."

"Felt like a damned fool," Randall admitted.

"You take my word for it," Temple said. "You did the right thing. Right down the line." He gave Randall another thump and started down the street in the direction Almquist had taken.

"I'll stay right here," Randall called, and Temple waved that he had heard.

Almquist had turned in at the hotel, but he stopped with one foot on the steps; his daughter had stepped out and she looked at him and smiled and said, "Hello, daddy. I'm married." She turned her head to look back at Ken Wallace, who was just coming through the door and she didn't see Almquist raise the flat of his hand.

She was just suddenly slapped and knocked asprawl and Jim Temple stopped and Ken Wallace stared at his new wife, then looked up, puzzled, angry, and yet holding it all back. "What shall I do, Mr. Temple?"

"You do what's right, boy."

Wallace nodded, then slowly turned his head and stared at Fred Almquist. Then he uncoiled like a bound spring, leaping on Almquist, bearing him staggering back. Almquist tripped on the top step and went down the flight backward with Wallace wrapped up with him like tangled yarn. The violence of the fall made Jim Temple wince and a crowd gathered on the run; the start of a fight was as good as a sounded dinner bell.

Almquist got to his feet first and mauled Wallace with his fist, but the young man got up, seeming to bounce like a flung rubber ball. Blood streamed down his nose and he charged Almquist, completely fearless, and was promptly knocked asprawl again.

224

Gena bounded off the porch; she would have tried to stop it had not Temple grabbed her around the waist and lifted her off the ground, kicking and yelling to be put down. He squeezed her hard enough to make her catch her breath and said, "Let them settle it, Gena. It's the only way. Do you understand? That's the only way."

She nodded and he put her down. Almquist was a man on the rampage; he was swinging wildly, yelling, stamping his feet, kicking, knocking young Wallace down, but Wallace always got up again. His face was battered and bloody and one eye was closed, but he still came after Almquist and it was something to see because Almquist just couldn't seem to stop him, seem to hit him hard enough or squarely enough.

The banker was slowing down and his breathing was labored now and sweat soaked his shirt and one sleeve dangled in shreds and his knees were turning watery. Still Wallace came at him and Almquist would beat him back and think that it was done and then Wallace would painfully get to his feet.

"Why don't you stay down?" Almquist asked, ripping the words out.

"You ain't gonna lick him," one man said and Almquist looked around as though to see who would dare put into words what he already knew.

Wallace was almost blind; he groped for the hitchrack and followed it a foot or two to get his bearings, then he came after Fred Almquist again, and this time Almquist put up his hands, but he backed up.

"You keep away," he said, backing into the crowd.

Jim Temple laid his voice on them like a hand. "Let him through. Let him run. Can't you see that he couldn't lick Wallace with a hammer?"

They parted and Fred Almquist stumbled through; he fell before he reached the walk but got up and ran a jagged path down the street.

Hands reached for Wallace, rough, work-stiff hands that were suddenly gentle and they carried him the few doors down to Dr. Chianti's office and up the stairs as though he were a fallen champion who must be healed quickly because his blood was theirs, his pain their pain and they could not stand the suffering.

Gena was crying and Temple gave her his handkerchief and made her blow her nose. "You've married yourself a man, Gena. I know more than a few women who can't say that."

"I hate my father," she said.

"No, you don't. Neither does Ken. But I'll tell you this: you won't have any more trouble from your dad. I'll bet too that he calls Ken 'Mr. Wallace' from now on."

She looked at him, then smiled. "You're good, Jim. I mean that."

"Why don't you go on up to him? Go on."

He watched her; she nodded, then dashed up the

steps. The crowd was still gathered, but Temple looked at them, slowly turning his head, and they remembered other places they'd rather be.

He crossed over to the phone company office and went in; three girls worked the switchboard and the supervisor came up, a woman of fifty who had long ago demonstrated tendencies toward strong will.

"No one but—"

"—phone company employees are allowed; yes, I know," Temple finished for her and irritated her no end. "However, I wish to make a phone call from this office on official business for the State of Texas." He smiled and some of her annoyance melted. "Naturally, I come to you, since you're the boss."

"Well, rules are made to be broken, they say. Whom did you want to call?"

"Spindle Ranch."

Someone on a party line was disconnected and then the supervisor put through his call. It took a few minutes to get Shannon to the telephone, then Temple said, "Al? Jim. I'd like to deputize Hobo Teal and another man. I'll let Hobo pick the second man, but he's got to be coolheaded and reliable."

"How about my youngest boy, Race?"

"Fine. Can they report to me at the jail in the morning?"

"Sure," Shannon said and hung up. Temple

handed the headset to the supervisor, then before she could think to react, he kissed her on the cheek. "You are sweet," he said, wrinkling his nose.

"Well for heaven's sake," she said as he went out the door, then the operators made the mistake of giggling and spent a trying hour while the supervisor's temper cooled.

Senator Lon Barrett read the paper the moment it hit the street, which was around six o'clock that evening, and then he went to Fred Almquist's house, called him an unbecoming name and hit him in the mouth, a thing which excited Mrs. Almquist no end and brought Fred Almquist out as far as his front gate, screaming threats and shaking his fist at Barrett's retreating figure.

Sheriff Hub Riley returned to town, getting off a cattle train that was whistle-stopped to let him off. He was a badly used man, limping along as he made his way to Thelma Scanlon's palace of solace. Jim Temple observed Riley's arrival and put the constable on him, warning him not to let Riley out of his sight, but not to follow him inside Thelma Scanlon's bawdy house.

Then he had one of those strokes of luck that come to a man once in awhile; Hobo Teal and Race Shannon had decided not to wait until morning and found Temple walking back toward the jail.

Race Shannon was slender, like his father, and he had the old man's gravity of expression. Temple ushered them inside and said, "I want to make you special deputies. I've got a feeling that the senator is going to find that ten-fifteen train for San Antone tonight almost too much to resist. Hobo, I want you stationed at the depot to see that he doesn't leave."

"I can do that. Where is he now?"

"Hotel." Temple glanced at young Shannon. "I'm going to put you outside Almquist's house. I don't want anything to happen to him, and he's not allowed to travel either."

"Will do," Shannon said. "Swear us in."

The procedure was simple; they took an oath of office, swore to defend the laws of the State of Texas, and he gave them deputy sheriff's badges, then sent them out on duty.

Still it didn't ease the growing concern in Temple's mind; he was like a man holding good cards and yet suspecting strongly that he was beaten. After thinking about it a moment, he sat down at the desk and cranked the handle on the telephone, asked for Judge Hanlon's home and got him.

"Jim Temple, sir. I hate to ask you this, but can you push up that meeting to tonight. Yes, sir, I know, but I've got some chickens flapping around and they're ready to fly the coop. Yes, sir, I'll need a court order and I'll see that they're served right away." He listened for a moment.

"All right, judge, in your office in fifteen minutes."

He hung up the phone then went back into the cell block, rattling the keys while he selected the one that opened the Adams' cell. He flung the door wide and said, "Boys, this will be your last night in jail if you do what I say. You walk out the front door, turn right and go around the building to the front of the courthouse. Up one flight of stairs and that's Judge Hanlon's chamber. You go in there and sit down. Now you do that and you'll all be free men before midnight. You run and you'll spend a lot of time behind bars."

Woody Adams said, "I sure don't understand this, Temple."

"No, and I don't have time to explain it to you. I'm going to put handcuffs on you so it'll look all right, but you do as I say. How about it?"

Otis shrugged. "Far as I'm concerned, we've got everything to gain by goin' along with you, Temple. You've got my word." He looked at his brothers. "How about it?"

They nodded and Temple motioned for them to step out. They went ahead of him to the front office and he took handcuffs out of the drawer and snapped them on their wrists, then dropped the key in Woody's pocket.

"What's that for?"

"Good faith. It proves I have it, and if you do like I said when you could unlock those 'cuffs and run for it, it'll prove yours once and for all."

He opened the front door. "Now get along. It's goin' to be a busy night for all of us."

"Man, just smell that fresh air," Woody said and grinned as he stepped out. They went around the side of the building and Temple hurried over to the hotel, checking with the clerk to get Stanley Franklin's room number.

Franklin was in, reading the paper; he answered the door then stepped back but Temple didn't come in. "Be in Judge Hanlon's chambers in an hour," Temple said.

"What for?"

"The judge will tell you."

Franklin shrugged. "I could make you get an order."

"Mister, there's one being written out right now. I'm just giving you a chance to be a volunteer."

"In that case I can't refuse," Franklin said and got his coat.

Judge Hanlon was a little surprised to find the Adams brothers waiting in his chambers, but he was becoming accustomed to odd doings and said nothing about it. Temple brought Franklin over and the lawyer sat down. Hanlon gave Temple his summons, one for each and Temple hurried out.

He found both Hobo Teal and Race Shannon with no difficulty and gave them each a summons. "Serve 'em," he said. "Take them right to the judge's chambers."

Then he backtracked across town to Thelma Scanlon's place. There was a piano going and a woman laughing; the parlor was crowded with men who had wives at home and they didn't like it because Jim Temple saw them there.

"Where's Riley?" he asked and one of the girls rolled her eyes upward and Temple took the stairs two at a time. At the landing he had three doors to choose from, but then he heard Riley laugh and opened the one on the right. The man had Thelma on his lap and a drink in his hand and his pistol laying on the dresser; he'd been caught cold and he knew it.

"Get over to the courthouse right away," Temple said. "Judge Hanlon's office. Relax, Riley, I didn't come here to make trouble for you. Bygones are bygones with me, unless you want to fly down these stairs too."

Riley pushed the woman off his lap and gathered up his gunbelt and hat. He stepped out ahead of Temple; they went down the stairs and outside.

"What's goin' on?"

"Damned if I know," Temple lied. "I follow orders the same as you do."

When they reached the courthouse, Riley went on inside. Hobo Teal was coming toward the steps with Senator Barrett in tow; the senator was carrying his suitcases and he stopped, glowering.

"This is a damned outrage."

Temple ignored him. "Where's the woman, Hobo?"

"He was alone. Come on there, sport. We wouldn't want to be late now."

"Wait a minute," Temple said. "Aren't you goin' to get married after all, senator?"

"To that slut? I know what she did. She told me." He shook off Temple's hand and marched up the steps. Temple followed them inside and saw that everyone was present.

Judge Hanlon sat on the bench and the Adams brothers and Hub Riley occupied the front row. Franklin and Almquist sat at the defense table and Hobo Teal pushed Lon Barrett along and made him sit there too.

Then the door opened and Al Shannon and his daughter came in, followed by Martha Ivers and Tom Keefer. Judge Hanlon smiled dryly and said, "My, we're going to have a cozy little gathering here, aren't we?" Then his eyes widened in surprise as Ken Wallace and Gena came in and took seats in back. "Sergeant Temple, have you invited the town?"

"I think that will be all, Your Honor. May I explain all this?"

"I do wish someone would," Hanlon admitted.

"Do you have the package, sir?"

Hanlon reached down out of sight and thumped it.

Temple faced them, standing with his back to the bench. "Your Honor, in about a week now you're going to preside over a case; the charge is bank robbery and murder, but you'll be asked to dismiss the murder charge in exchange for the guilty plea on the robbery. The only thing wrong with it is that the Adams boys didn't do it at all. As a matter of fact, judge, there wasn't really a robbery, because the money never left the bank. Now I'm givin' this to you kind of fast but when the charges are formally made, I'm in a position to prove everything I say. Fact is, I'm going to prove it tonight, right here.

"Now Fred Almquist has a very bad habit and that's robbin' his own banks. I think it all started in Oklahoma, but it's my feelin' that he didn't have anything to do with it there. He was robbed all right, cleaned out, and that's enough to discourage any banker. Then along comes a fella with money and an idea and Almquist listens, takes the money and comes here, only to be robbed again. Only this time it's in his favor and there's a split, between the robber and the backer and Fred Almquist." He pointed at Almquist. "Here's the banker." Then he swung his finger to Lon Barrett, "—and the backer, and Hub Riley, the man who hit Ken Wallace over the head. Judge, there were only two people in the bank that day. That is, two in front and Riley who was let in the back way. He hit Wallace, then Almquist locked the money in Wallace's drawer and let Riley out the back again. The bound and gagged business was just part of the show; Almquist really wasn't tied up at all." He turned and glanced at the judge. "Would you read the letter that is sealed to the box, judge?"

"Delighted. I must tell all this to my wife; she thinks my cases are dull." He tore open the letter, peeling back the wax, and began to read.

We, the undersigned, do swear that the contents of the attached package was taken from the cashier's drawer of The Citizens Bank, counted twice, placed in the package and sealed, and thereafter, until deposited in Judge Hanlon's safe keeping, was not out of sight or hand. The contents of this package will be displayed in a constituted court.

Signed: Al Shannon
Tom Keefer
James Temple

"Would you now open the package, Your Honor?"

Hanlon did, then stacked the eighteen thousand, one hundred and eight dollars where they all could see it. Jim Temple said, "There's the loot from the robbery sir, and it never left the bank until it was recovered by a duly constituted officer of the law."

"You broke into my bank!" Almquist screamed and jumped up and Lon Barret promptly knocked him down.

"Shut up, you idiot," Barrett said tightly.

"Your Honor," Temple said, "I would like to see the court move to dismiss the charges against Woody Adams, Otis Adams, and Marvin Adams. I realize that the court is not in session but—"

"It is if I say it is, and I say it is. The charges are dismissed."

"I would like to see the court," Temple went on, "hold Fred Almquist and Lon Barrett on charges of conspiracy to defraud."

"They will be held in custody until the grand jury can convene," Hanlon said. "They are remanded to custody."

Hub Riley, a man who never really liked to wait for anything, decided that this was the time to move; he bolted out of his chair and before he could take one step, Woody Adams was on him, his handcuffs around Riley's throat, bearing him to the floor, choking the life out of him.

Hobo Teal moved in and took over, disarming Riley and slamming him back in the chair. "Sorry for the interruption," he said.

Temple said, "Judge, Riley killed Morgan, and maybe we can't prove that, but we can prove that he has robbed the bank for Almquist and Barrett."

"Placed in custody," Hanlon said. He looked at Stanley Franklin, then at Temple. "What about him?"

"I leave that up to you, sir."

"Now I appreciate that," Hanlon said in a chilly voice. "Approach the bench, please." He bored holes into Stanley Franklin with his eyes. "Now listen carefully. I believe I could substantiate very serious charges against you which would result in your disbarment. However I'm going to warn you to be extremely careful in the future. This will get around so I would not take this lightly. Now get the hell out of my court and my county."

Franklin bowed with mock gravity and clapped on his hat. He looked at Jim Temple a moment, then said, "You cheap tinstar, you were lucky." Then he shouldered out, slamming the door.

Temple made a motion to Teal and young Shannon. "All right, get this tribe of upright citizens out of here." He looked at Woody Adams and smiled. "Go ahead and use that key now."

Hanlon was a little surprised at this move. He frowned and said, "Sergeant, breaking into the bank, and now permitting prisoners to carry the key to their own handcuffs?" He shook his head. "Next thing you'll be advocating going to the zoo and giving the monkeys the right to vote on whether they should have their cages unlocked or not."

"Yes, sir. I sure stand corrected, sir."

"The hell you do," Hanlon said, smiling.

"There's just one more thing, judge."

"Another favor?"

"Well, yes, sir."

"All right, what is it this time?" He sounded a bit weary.

"Well, we've given these three men a pretty rough time of it. Now they've got no kind of a record at all, and they need work, and since you're without a sheriff, I sort of thought—"

"You did?"

"Yes, sir."

"All by yourself?" He looked severely at Temple, then nodded. "We'll work something out, sergeant. And I think it's a good thing." He stood up, packing the money back in the box. "Now may I go home and worry about someone stealing this?"

Temple was through and it was like a sigh running through him, a good thing, a relief. Woody Adams and his brothers crowded around him and Woody said, "Jim, we won't ever forget this."

"Now I didn't plan to let you. I'll be getting back this way once in awhile and I'll look you up for a free meal. After all, you county lawmen make all the money and split the fines." He slapped Woody on the arm and went to the back of the room.

Nora Shannon waited there. She touched him on the arm and he stopped. "I suppose they'll confess now?"

"Sure. They'll figure the first one who talks will get a lighter sentence. That kind either has to be stealing something or trying to buy their way out."

"I was going to tell them," she said. "And now I

won't have to. I suppose I have it coming, not being able to make a clean—"

"They don't need to know," Temple said. Al Shannon was standing there like a fence post with snow on top, listening, wondering, but staying out of it. "Nora, the thing that matters is that you would have spoken. That's the important thing. Don't you see that?"

She raised her eyes like a person with few wits, then a light came into them and she smiled. "Why, that's true, isn't it?"

"Sure as rain."

"Jim, I can live again, can't I?"

"It's a big jolly world," he said. "Just look around your own backyard for the answer."

"Hobo?"

"See, you've noticed already." He gave her cheek a gentle pat and went outside and found Tom Keefer hunkered down on the bottom step.

"What's next?" Keefer asked.

"Put me up for the night?"

"Thought I was in for a touch," Keefer grumbled.
"You're goin' to need a housekeeper."

"Thought that too," Keefer said and got up. "Well, let's go if we're goin'. I need my sleep. Farmin's hard work." Then he turned and laughed and put his hands to his stomach. "Oh, ain't you some punkins? You really are the berries." He was laughing when he went after the horses.

Center Point Large Print
600 Brooks Road / PO Box 1
Thorndike ME 04986-0001 USA

(207) 568-3717

US & Canada:
1 800 929-9108
www.centerpointlargeprint.com